CENTERED

GOLD HOCKEY #9

ELISE FABER

CENTERED
BY ELISE FABER
Newsletter sign-up

CENTERED
Copyright © 2020 Elise Faber
Print ISBN-13: 978-1-946140-74-6
Ebook ISBN-13: 978-1-946140-73-9
Cover Art by Jena Brignola

GOLD HOCKEY SERIES

Gold Hockey **(all stand alone)**
Blocked
Backhand
Boarding
Benched
Breakaway
Breakout
Checked
Coasting
Centered
Charging
Caged
Crashed
A Gold Christmas
Cycled
Caught
Cap

Gold Cast of Characters

Heroes and Heroines:

Brit Plantain (Blocked) — first female goalie in the NHL, loves boy bands

Stefan Barie (Blocked) — captain of the Gold

Sara Jetty (Backhand) — artist and figure skater

Mike Stewart (Backhand) —defenseman for the Gold, romance guru

Blane Hart (Boarding) — center for the Gold, number 22

Mandy Shallows (Boarding) — trainer and physical therapist

Max Montgomery (Benched) — defensemen for the Gold, giant nerd

Angelica Shallows (Benched) — engineer at RoboTech, also a giant nerd

Blue Anderson (Breakaway) — top forward in the league and for the Gold

Anna Hayes (Breakaway) — Max's former nanny, no relation to Kevin Hayes

Rebecca Stravokraus (Breakout) — Gold publicist, makes killer brownies, known at PR-Rebecca

Kevin Hayes (Breakout) — forward for the Gold, no relation to Anna Hayes

Rebecca Hallbright (Checked) — nutritionist for the Gold, plethora of delicious vegan recipes, known as Nutrionist-Rebecca

Gabe Carter (Checked) — doctor, head trainer for the Gold

Calle Stevens (Coasting) — assistant coach for the Gold, former national team member

Coop Armstrong (Coasting) — talented forward on the Gold, addicted to historical romance audiobooks

Mia Caldwell (Centered) — 5th degree black belt, brings the snark

Liam Williamson (Centered) — Gold forward finding his love for the game, charming and pushy in equal measures

Charlotte Harris (Charging) — new Gold GM, hates losing and the game Chubby Bunny

Logan Walker (Charging) — defensemen for the Gold, skills include: cockiness and being able to buy presents that make Charlotte squirm

Devon Scott (Block & Tackle) — former player, current owner Prestige Media group

Becca Scott (Block & Tackle) — Devon's assistant

Additional Characters:

Bernard — head coach

Richie — equipment manager

Dan Plantain — Brit's brother

Diane Barie — Stefan's mom

Pierre Barie — Stefan's dad, owner of the Gold

Spence — former goalie, married to Monique, daughter Mirabel

Monique — married to Spence, former model

Mirabel — daughter of Spence and Monique

Mitch — Sara's boss

Allison and Sean — Blane's parents

Pascal — Devon Scott's security lead

Roger Shallows — Mandy's dad

Grant and Megan — Devon's parents

ONE

LIAM

He was fucking up.

As usual.

He'd had a particularly bad practice, after a particularly bad game, after a particularly bad *series* of games, and he knew that his hopes of staying with the San Francisco Gold were quickly becoming slim-to-none.

The name Williamson used to strike fear in the league.

His grandfather, his father, his two older brothers all had been forces to be reckoned with.

He . . . was scraping by.

Four teams in four seasons.

Shitty stats.

And somehow, he'd gotten picked up off waivers by the Gold, reigning league champions, who were in the midst of a rebuilding season after losing some of their big stars to retirement.

He was expected to fill a hole.

But how in the fuck was *he*, the smallest and least scary of the Williamsons, supposed to fill a hole when he'd barely earned a roster spot?

Fuck.

He put his head down, tugged the collar of his jacket up.

He should just call it already, put the league behind him and find a new career. Math had been his strong suit—maybe he should go back and be an accountant. He could run his brothers' multimillion-dollar fortunes, help them eke out a few more dollars and—

"Watch out!"

The warning came a second too late.

He'd already stepped off the curb, already put himself in range of the car that was blowing through the red light, tearing through the intersection, not giving a shit that there were pedestrians walking—

Well, of all the ways to go, at least this would be quick.

But just as the car came within an inch of him, Liam found himself jerked back onto the curb, his one-hundred-and-eighty-pound frame becoming unwieldy and clumsy.

Kind of like on the ice over the last few years.

That was his last thought before he found himself sprawled, ass first, on the San Franciscan sidewalk.

Gross.

"What. The. *Fuck?*" a female voice snapped.

The same female voice that had warned him.

"Do you have a fucking death wish?" she yelled, causing his eyes to snap open, making him look up at an angel . . . a foot tapping, arms crossed, seriously pissed, and seemingly way too small to have been able to haul his ass back onto the curb female.

Liam thought he just might have that death wish.

Especially if it meant he got to be rescued by a woman who looked like an angel. He opened his mouth to reply.

But apparently didn't work fast enough.

Because the woman, the beautiful, curvy female, made a disgusted noise and strode away from him.

He watched her go, watched that gorgeous ass stride down the sidewalk, and stop outside a storefront. By the time he pushed to his feet, she'd pulled out her keys and unlocked the door, disappearing inside.

Liam glanced at the sign overhead.

Golden Gate Martial Arts.

He thought of the swaying hips as she'd stomped away. He thought of the fiery words she'd snapped at him. He thought of the pretty brown eyes and lush lips incongruously paired with enough strength to pull him out of the way of the oncoming car.

And suddenly, he thought that, hockey or not, he might just want to stay in San Francisco after all.

Two

MIA

She leaned back against the closed door, hand pressed to her chest as her heart threatened to beat its way out of her body.

Her pulse pounded, her free hand shook, her legs were weak.

"What the fuck?" she muttered, sinking down onto the floor, dropping her forehead to her bent knees.

The cars. The horn. The man . . . standing in the middle of the crosswalk.

Not moving.

Not *fucking* moving.

She could still feel the heat of the car's engine as it barreled toward him, toward her, when she'd run forward to pull him back. Adrenaline had made her fast and strong, had allowed her to get them both onto the sidewalk. That, paired with the car swerving enough to avoid them at the last minute, had meant she hadn't ended up a San Franciscan pancake.

And now, she had to teach karate to a group of four-year-olds.

Mia sat there for a few minutes, thankful she'd been running ahead of schedule but cognizant that her window to get her shit together was closing. In fifteen minutes, her kiddos would start showing up for their thirty-minute class of jumping, kicking, yelling, and rolling.

All controlled, of course. One of the reasons she loved this sport so much was that every movement, every yell, every kick and punch *and* roll were to demonstrate some aspect of control.

Although, she thought, pushing herself to her feet and taking some slow deep breaths, that control was relative when it came to four-year-olds.

"Better," she murmured, the adrenaline surge gone, the shaking diminishing.

Now, she could focus enough to review her lesson plan, to set up for class. She moved to her ever-present clipboard, the one with all of her class information, and the one she would be totally lost without. Finding today's sheet, she saw she would have some helpers, but they were ten and twelve, and students in her program for older kids. Brayden and Will were focused and respectful, but they were still ten and twelve.

Juggling.

Most of her job was juggling.

Lips curving upward into a smile, a large grin that would ruin her tough-as-nails persona if anyone saw, she thought of how much she enjoyed juggling. Nothing made her happier than when she was managing several things at once, when she had more than a handful of balls in the air.

Handful of balls.

Heh.

But inner dirty mind aside, multitasking was her superpower.

Running a class of wiggly kids while also answering the occasional phone call, fielding questions from parents, keeping an eye on her assistants . . . and that was all just during one class. Then rinse and repeat for all of the other classes—which, on any given evening, could number five.

But she loved it.

She loved kids. She loved teaching. She loved the connection the studio gave her to her dad.

What she *didn't* enjoy was the knock on the door precisely ten minutes before class started, just as she was pulling out the pads she'd need for the lesson. Sighing, juggling the pads—more juggling, *ha*—as she made her way over to the door, she flicked open the lock and nudged the door outward, her teacher voice already prepped and ready since her students knew better than to knock, knew they were supposed to wait outside until she invited them into the studio.

"Remember—"

Her admonishment cut off because standing outside the door was . . . *him.*

The stranger she'd pulled from the crosswalk, the one who'd sprawled with her on the concrete of the sidewalk, who'd twisted slightly to take the brunt of the fall, even as she'd braced herself for the impact that was coming.

He was big . . . and pretty.

Deep gray eyes, so dark they almost looked black. Rich tan skin that hinted at Mediterranean roots and made her mouth water for pasta, her stomach yearn for pizza, though she rarely indulged in junk food. Long lashes, a plump bottom lip, a crisp jawline. His nose had a bump along its bridge, indicating it had been broken before, but that along with other signs of imperfection scattered across his face only somehow added to the pretty— scars forming an X bisecting his right brow, another near the corner of his mouth, one more marring a spot halfway along his jaw.

Beautiful, but not perfect. Gorgeous in the imperfections.

Desire, hot and heady, swept through her.

And Mia got pissed.

She might enjoy multitasking, might in some darkly logical portion of her mind be able to attribute juggling attraction with the duties of her job, with the promises she'd made herself as the ultimate form of multitasking. But the heat that had swept through her at the sight of this man in the street, the flames that burst back into life when her gaze met his now, told her that rationalizing the way her body paid attention to this man's was not going to go well. It undermined. It made her want things she'd carefully boxed up and tucked away.

She dealt in control, not in waves of lust, not in the intense desire this man had invoked in just a few seconds, her body instantly attuned to the beautiful man inches from her, remembering the way he'd felt pressed against her, cradling her against the impact, at least until she'd remembered herself.

Because fuck, she needed to get laid.

A slow, hot smile turned up the edges of that luscious mouth, and Mia thought for a second she'd said that aloud. Thankfully, as the silence stretched, as no pithy comment emerged, it seemed she hadn't. Instead, she watched his smile widen as he traced his gaze from her face—hair now pulled back into a severe ponytail, to her *gi*, crisp white and tied with her fifth-degree black belt, down to her bare toes.

"Fifth-degree?" he asked, and she barely held back the shiver his voice had sliding down her spine.

Deep. Velvet, with a hint of rasp.

Pure sex.

Stifling the intense heat that flashed through her, that slid between her thighs, that had moisture pooling there, she simply lifted a brow.

Yes, she was fifth-degree, and nearly twenty years of work had gone into that thick band of embroidered black cotton.

She resisted the urge to cross her arms as his gaze dipped down again.

"You look about fourteen," he muttered.

"I'm twenty-six," she said. "What about you?" She let her gaze glide deliberately to his temples, to the gray strands threaded there. "Forty?"

Another hot smile that had the hairs on her nape standing up. But this one was paired with a shake of his head, a step forward.

"Actually, I started going gray at eighteen," he said, voice dropping, getting even huskier.

"So, you're what then?" Mia said, taking a deliberate step backward, moving into the studio, letting go of the door. He caught it before it closed on him, broad fingers wrapping around the metal frame as she came to a stop a couple feet away, both unnerved by this man and confident she'd be able to defend herself if the need arose. "Twenty?"

The man stayed in place, just on the threshold of the door. "Twenty-five."

So young for such heavy secrets in his soft gray eyes. But then again, Mia knew her own eyes held plenty of secrets, plenty of pain.

Not going there.

She lifted her chin. "Did you have a reason for knocking on my door?"

"*Your* door?" he asked, lifting his brow but not moving any closer.

"This is my studio," she said.

"Impressive."

No. It had begun as an obsession—to not let go of this last tie to her father—then it had broken and reformed into something that was more obligation than connection, and finally . . . it had become part of her. Something she loved and lived for.

"What do you want?" she asked.

A blunt question, but that was Mia.

Sharp and to the point. No fluff. But also the perfect way to keep people at a distance with her off-putting frankness.

The man blinked, face showing surprise with her tone. Yet, he didn't retreat, didn't react like most men who approached her did —he certainly didn't back up, didn't flee under the intensity of her direct stare.

Instead, his lips curved slightly, the barest bend softening the corners of his mouth, drawing her focus, making her mouth water.

Making her brain struggle to refocus.

Thankfully, she'd had twenty years of training that helped her to concentrate through distractions. Which meant she was able to shove down the attraction and wait him out.

The brow came down, the mouth flattened, seriousness took over mischief.

"I wanted to say thank you," he said. "I—" Something dark flashed through his expression. "Thank you for rescuing me. You shouldn't have put your life at risk to save mine."

"It wasn't a big deal."

"No."

She tilted her head to the side at the sharp tone, surprised it had come from him and not her own mouth.

"It *was* a huge deal," he said and then muttered, almost to himself, "I risked a stranger's life and nearly got myself run over because I couldn't get out of my head." His eyes made him seem far away even though they never left hers, and Mia found herself frozen in place. Then he blinked, and he was right there in the present. "I'm sorry."

Two simple words filled with such intensity.

"You're welcome."

She thought she'd surprised him with the reply, but what was she supposed to say? *It's okay?* It *wasn't* okay. The blasted man nearly had gotten himself flattened on the street. And her, for that matter. Though she only could reasonably blame herself for that.

If she hadn't pulled him back—

No. Now was not the time to think about losing people, whether it was a stranger or a loved one. Mia straightened her shoulders, snapped, "Well, don't expect me to do it again." With that, she turned away and began to lay out the pads, one in each delineated square on the foam mat. She needed to stop chatting and start getting ready for her class. "Keep your head up, check for traffic before you enter a crosswalk, and always be aware of your surroundings."

She was aware of him shifting, the door closing behind him. "Is that what you tell your kids?"

It was. But he didn't need to know that.

Her eyes tracked his movements through the mirrors at the front, along the sides of the studio, and so she saw when he took a step forward, shoes mere inches from her mat.

"Freeze," she snapped, whirling to face him, pointer finger in full force.

Two brown brows lifted, but he dutifully stopped. "Is there a reason I'm playing statue?" he asked dryly after a few seconds.

"Do not take one step onto my mat with those dirty shoes."

Those brows went higher.

Then he shifted, one foot going behind the other as he toed off one sneaker then the remaining. He made as though to step forward again then stopped, eyes coming to hers. When she didn't order him to *Freeze* again, he walked onto the mat and crossed over to her, reaching for the pads in her arms. "I can lay these out for you," he said.

She resisted the urge to hug them against her chest, not wanting to let this man get close, to touch things that belonged to her, and definitely not wanting his help.

He knew it. One or all three, she couldn't be sure, but somehow, even though she deliberately flicked her eyes to the mirror, checked her face was set into the blank teacher mask that always got her kids to behave, this man knew she wanted to refuse.

His smile was knowing, his eyes soft. "I've made you late," he cajoled. "Let me help."

The mental war took all of three more seconds.

She *was* running late.

And multitasking was easier with help.

"Fine," she said, well aware that her tone still bordered on snap. "Lay one out in each square then also grab three blockers— the long foam stick with the black handles—and six large pads and stack them near the front."

He nodded, seemingly unperturbed by both her orders and

her sharp voice. After placing the pads, he moved to the storage shelves on the left side of the studio that held all sorts of equipment they used for classes. Confident he was following instructions, she grabbed her clipboard, refreshed her brain for the day's curriculum, and snagged the electronic tablet the kids used to check in, bringing it to the small table by the entrance that had a plug for the tablet (no running out of power on her watch), and a bottle of hand sanitizer.

The kids—*not* the parents, because she was trying to do her part in raising confident, capable kids—cleaned their hands, then found their name on the roster for their rank, and checked themselves in before stowing their shoes in the cubbies and lining up on the floor. Then would come a warm-up, stretching, a quick talk (very quick and age-appropriate for this group of four-year-olds) on the week's life-related subject—the current topic being what to do if a stranger approached. After that, they would kick and punch and yell, and then wrap up the thirty minutes with her version of Simon Says.

She was just plugging in the tablet when the door swung open and Brayden came in, his equipment bag that was nearly as big as him hanging from his shoulder. "Hi, Ms. Caldwell."

"Hi, Mr. Montgomery," she said. "Drop your stuff and help with the equipment."

"Yes, ma'am."

She tapped the pin code to open the screen, pulled up the rosters for the classes, and was just setting it down when she heard him exclaim, "*Liam?*"

Spinning, she saw Brayden had stopped a few feet away from the man she'd pulled off the street and realized she'd been dumb to not identify the man as one of the new players picked up by the San Francisco Gold. In fact, she'd watched him play in the last game, bullied into accepting a ticket to watch the team from Brayden's professional hockey player dad, Max.

As a player, Liam was smooth and strong, but struggling to adjust to a new team.

In his head. Struggling. Oncoming traffic.

Hmm.

Liam set down the last of the large pads and turned to Brayden. "Hey, man," he said, extending his hand and executing some sort of complicated handshake. "A black belt, huh? That's awesome."

Brayden nodded eagerly. "Ms. Caldwell is the best. She's really tough, and I've seen her kick so high she could almost touch the ceiling."

Liam's eyes flicked from Brayden to her to said ceiling. "Flexible as well as strong then, huh?"

Brayden nodded when Liam glanced back at him. "Yup. Ms. Caldwell says flexibility is really important."

"Well, Ms. Caldwell is right about that." Liam straightened.

"Ms. Caldwell is always right," Brayden said as he made his way over to the clipboard. She wanted to reprimand him for talking but refrained. They usually chatted as they set up for class, and he was doing everything exactly as she expected. "No, we need the large blockers," Brayden said when Liam reached onto the wrong shelf and before she could correct him. "Not the medium ones."

The only difference was instead of chatting with her or Will—who was just walking through the door, a quiet, "Hi, Ms. Caldwell," drifting to her ears—Brayden was talking to the gorgeous, unnerving Liam Williamson—professional hockey player, the sexy and lean pretty-boy new addition to the Gold she'd just snatched out of the path of a car. So, instead of snapping at the child she'd been teaching for close to five years now, she finished the rest of her prep while listening to them talk about the Gold's upcoming games.

She was just reaching for the handle, readying to push open the door when she heard it.

"Are you taking classes here?" Brayden asked.

Her gaze shot over her shoulder, locked with Liam's and saw the mischief bleed into his face.

Fucking hell.

No. He *wouldn't*.

He. Wouldn't.

She narrowed her eyes, gave him the ultimate Ms. Caldwell Death Glare.

Liam just grinned.

"No, bud," he said. "No classes."

Mia released a long, relieved breath then pushed open the door. Time for—

"Ms. Caldwell is giving me private lessons."

THREE

LIAM

He was sitting in the corner of the studio, alternating between being impressed by the woman, a little scared, and more turned on than he'd ever been in his life.

The last was a problem because there were children around.

So, Liam had deliberately thought not about the way the white *gi* pants Ms. Caldwell was wearing clung to muscular thighs, swept over the delicious curves of her ass. He still didn't know her first name, and all of the naughty schoolboy, teacher/student fantasies he'd had during his younger years were loving that fact. *He*, the adult male that occasionally made its presence known inside him, was less inclined to be popping a boner, especially considering the fact that her bending over was to help a kid who looked all of twelve with the positioning of his foot during a kick.

Brayden, Max's son, had left about an hour before, after helping with two classes and taking his own. He'd barreled out the door with an equipment bag the size of an elephant dangling from his shoulder.

Now, Liam glanced at his cell. It was nearing eight, Ms. Caldwell hadn't missed a beat, and despite making his livelihood as a professional athlete, he was a little exhausted from watching her.

Although, that could also be because he'd barely slept the night before.

Wondering about hockey, about his future, about the messages on his cell from his brothers and father. Well-meaning and encouraging texts from his brothers. Critiques about his play and suggestions to do better from his father.

All sitting unread, the little red circle numbering nine in the upper righthand corner of the messaging app on his cell taunting him with every minute that passed.

He needed to read them.

He needed to *go.*

But he'd been fascinated watching Ms. Caldwell work. She was . . . absolute grace. Smooth and confident in her demonstrations, strong in voice, and demanding utter respect from the kids. Yet, his favorite thing he'd been able to witness was her humor. Small little jokes the kids wouldn't pick up, but that the grownups did, earning a chuckle from the parents, from him.

Of course, when she heard *him* chuckle, her eyes narrowed, and she speared him in place with a ferocious glare.

Probably one that should have made his balls shrivel up.

Instead, it made his cock twitch.

Which then made him resort to thinking about those messages on his cell in order to control himself and not wonder if she'd use that sharp tone, those sharp words in bed.

He was waffling between opening the app and checking texts or ignoring them for the remainder of his time on this planet when he heard Ms. Caldwell ask everyone to stand, and directed the students in bowing out of class. Shortly after, the kids filed out, gathering shoes as they went, parents bundling them up in jackets to protect them from the winter breeze of a forthcoming storm making its way toward the Bay Area.

Liam had half-expected another class to file in, for Ms. Caldwell to go to her ever-trusty clipboard and gather supplies.

Instead, she answered a few questions from parents who lingered, hugged a teenage girl who seemed to be having a bad day, and then began taking pads down and spreading them out, wiping them efficiently with a disinfecting wipe.

He was on his feet before he thought about moving, toeing off his shoes without being asked this time, and walking over to the pads, picking up the ones that were dry and stacking them onto the shelves. "This okay?" he asked when she was nearly through with the row.

Her eyes, dark chocolate with flecks of hazelnut, met his for a long moment.

Then she nodded.

And something inside him relaxed. He brought the pads—smaller than the ones she'd just cleaned—down and lined them up to clean, switching places with her when she'd finished the first row to put those back up.

They repeated the process in silence. Her wiping them down, occasionally swapping out her dirty wipe for a clean one, him bringing the pads up and down on the shelves once they were dry. Him trying to ignore the way her ass looked glorious as she bent over in front of him. Her barely looking at him, definitely not noticing *his* ass.

It wasn't until he'd stacked the last pad that she spoke.

"What are you still doing here, Liam?"

But he could barely hear her words, not when the sight of her going up on tiptoe to stow the container of wipes had frozen him in place.

Bare feet with blue nail polish—because, of course, he'd noticed. Slender ankles, the right one with a thin gold chain wrapped around it, smooth olive skin, the loose pants of her *gi* tugging at all the spots on her legs that hinted at strength—her calves, her thighs—and juxtaposed by thin, almost fragile-looking wrists. Shining black hair that trailed down her back in a thick ponytail, cute ears (who knew he would ever think ears would be cute?), a tattoo behind her left ear that was small and tucked away, something he wouldn't have noticed if he hadn't found himself cataloging every *single* thing about this woman.

Obsessed.

It was how he, the smallest of all the Williamson brothers had gotten into the NHL in the first place, how he'd shattered the records in high school, in juniors.

When he loved something, he was obsessed.

Not that he loved this woman; he'd met her that day, didn't even know her name, but when he enjoyed something, when he was fascinated by it, and Liam strove to understand every bit of minutia that came along with the subject.

Skating.

Shooting.

Stickhandling.

Using differential equations in applied mathematics.

Ms. Caldwell.

Each required attention to detail in order to be successful. But only one was bordering on obsession.

Probably because it was mere hours old.

Probably because while math was interesting, he didn't want to spend his life with his nose in a book.

And probably also because somewhere along his transition from college to professional hockey, he'd lost his confidence. It hadn't come easy any longer, and God that sounded arrogant and egotistical, but the truth was that his playing in the NHL was harder than he'd ever expected.

And he was struggling big time.

Failing.

Big time.

"Liam?"

He blinked and tuned out of the thoughts in his head. "Sorry, what?"

"Why are you still here?" she asked, sharper now as she

dropped down onto the soles of her feet. Why did he like it so much when she snapped at him? Probably it said something bad about him, but all he could think was that he would love to hear her giving him those same terse orders in bed. "Why are you smiling?" she asked, eyes narrowed, feet silent as she crossed to him and plunked her hands onto her hips.

"No reason."

She huffed. "Sure." A roll of those pretty chocolate eyes. "No reason, my ass."

"It's a fine ass," he said.

She moved so fast that before he could process the movement, his wrist was caught in a lock that Liam knew if he moved a single muscle, the ligaments would tear, the bones would break. "You do *not* have permission to speak about my body that way."

He turned his head enough to meet her eyes. "Understood," he said calmly, even though he felt anything but. "My apologies."

She snorted. "I could end your season with the twitch of my pinky finger."

His heart thumped, but he couldn't decide if it was out of fear or anticipation. If he couldn't play the rest of the season, he might not have a chance to impress the Gold enough to keep him on for another season. But, on the other hand, if he couldn't play, maybe this would be the death knell on his career and force him to choose another route.

Maybe he could be free.

But . . . did he *want* to be free? Would he miss the game, the way the cold air of the rink seeped into his skin, bit at his nose? Would he long for the speed, the impact of the checks, the comraderie and competition?

He thought he would.

And so, Liam supposed he had a little bit of fight left in him.

Enough to at least say, "You're sexy when you're threatening me."

He half-expected to feel shooting pain, but instead she just released him, shaking her head as she returned to her little set of shelves on the edge of the floor and began filing some papers away.

"You know," he said, moving to the table to retrieve the tablet and bringing it to her, "You still haven't told me your first name, Ms. Caldwell."

Was there the barest hint of heat in her eyes?

Liam squinted, but it was gone before he could be sure, and anyway, then she was talking again, and the acerbic words were going straight to his cock. "You still haven't asked."

Going still for a few seconds, backtracking their conversations, he realized he *hadn't* asked, hadn't even introduced himself. If Brayden hadn't used their names, they would still effectively be the same strangers from the street. Except . . . not. Because this woman was—

More.

And he had the feeling she was *more* than anyone he'd ever met.

Reining himself in, he stuck out his hand for her to shake. "I'm Liam Williamson."

Her fingers brushed his first, sending sparks along his palm, up his arm. Then their hands were pressed together, and her grip was firm . . . and great, his cock was hard again. Going harder when she slipped her hand free, spun away, and said, "I know."

She strode to the door, pushed it open. "Goodnight, Mr. Williamson. Good luck with your season. I think the Gold might have another shot at the Cup this year."

He took a step, thinking to regroup and come up with a plan to get this woman to like him, to go out on a date with him, to kiss him. But also knowing that he needed to return another day to fight. Except . . . then his brain processed her words.

That was the second time she'd said *season*, and now she'd mentioned the Cup and the San Francisco Gold. She knew he played.

Liam hadn't told her that.

So she either followed the sport . . . or—

He didn't know. She was a stalker, somehow had tracked down all of the Williamsons and was ready to go puck bunny. Right. He stifled a snort. That was about as likely as him receiving the Hart Memorial Trophy.

As in, nonexistent.

But all he understood was that he didn't care how she seemed to know something about him, because the fact that she *did* made his heart leap and he wanted to share *all* the things, even knowing it was too much. Too fast. Too—

Insane.

He was being insane.

Yet, he found himself stopping on the mat, staying in place, asking, "How'd you know I play hockey?"

Still.

She could go so *freaking* still. A beautiful marble statue gilded gold from the overhead lights, a calm expression hiding so much underneath, all the strokes it took to create her, the chipping away of rock, the polishing of the rough spots. But even knowing it was all beneath the surface, he could only see the beauty on the outside.

"Ms. Caldwell," he prompted.

She startled, let the door slide shut and bent to pick up his shoes, shoving them into his chest. "You need to go."

He grabbed the sneakers by instinct, decided to take a different route with the questioning. Or maybe it was less conscious and more urge to bounce around subjects, wanting to know everything about her. "I thought I was coming for private lessons."

A roll of her eyes. "That's not happening."

"How'd you know I play for the Gold?"

"Brayden—"

He shook his head. He'd already run back through that conversation, knew Bray hadn't said anything about him being a hockey player. "No, that's not it," he murmured, taking a step toward her.

Her eyes narrowed and she huffed out a sigh. "I saw you play," she said. "Against St. Louis."

He didn't hide his wince, knowing that game had been one of his worst in recent years.

"What?" she asked. "I thought you played well. You're still getting your legs with being new to the team, learning the different system of play, of course, but you definitely have the potential to fit in and be a good asset."

Exactly what he'd heard . . . four times over.

Just give it time.

You'll slide into place.

It'll be fine. Just relax. Play your game.

And that was the moment everything became too much. He needed to get out of here. Because no matter how fascinating this woman was, he couldn't do this. Not again. Couldn't make ties, have hopes, desires, longing to find the spot where he belonged . . . because right around the corner, he might lose that again.

Liam knew he couldn't do it again.

He spun, strode for the end of the mat, dropping his shoes to the floor and sitting down in a chair to quickly put them on.

"What are you doing?"

Another sharp question and heaven help him, but he liked it too much. "Thanks again," he said, tying the laces on one tennis shoe then the other. He stood. "I—"

"My name is Mia."

Mia.

Her voice had come from right in front of him again, silent feet closing the distance between them.

His heart skipped a beat, and he looked from those midnight blue toes up into those dark chocolate eyes and knew that it was the perfect name. Mia.

Mine.

Mine.

"Mia," he whispered.

She was quiet for a few seconds then nodded. "Yes." A beat. "Why do you care that I saw you play?"

He let his gaze slide from hers, knew he was too weak to tell her the truth.

That he *wasn't* good, that he'd lost something along the way and his game hadn't recovered, and he was unsure if it ever would. Instead, he slid toward the door.

She made a sound, a disappointed sound, and he knew he'd failed some kind of test.

Hell, *that* was a familiar feeling.

But fuck, he hated the notion of failing this woman.

"I didn't take you for a coward," she said on a sigh, and this time, if he listened very carefully, he heard her feet shift, felt her start to move away.

Leaving him.

Fuck, he hated that, too.

Which was the moment he stopped thinking.

He reached out a hand, snagged her arm. "About those private less—*ah!*"

One second, he was on his feet, fingers wrapped around Mia's arm, reveling in how small it felt beneath his giant bear paws. The next, her elbow connected with his jaw and . . .

He was on his ass again. Well, sprawled out on his back, his lungs frozen for several heartbeats as the air was squeezed from them, the organs stunned into submission until finally, *finally,* he was able to suck in some oxygen.

She yanked his fingers from her arm, straightened, hands lifting to tidy her *gi* then said, "Consider that your first and only private lesson. Don't lay hands on women who don't give you permission."

Noted.

Fuck, but that was noted.

His already sore back and ass, from the impact earlier, were practically screaming in pain, and he knew his jaw would be sporting a giant bruise. But it wasn't so much the physical pain as . . . Liam was ashamed. "I'm sorry."

"Seems you're good at saying that," she muttered, reaching into a tiny office next to the cubbies where she kept her clipboard and files and retrieving a small bag. "But what you're not good at, clearly, is pairing actions with words."

A truer statement about his life had never been spoken.

So much promise.

So little to show for it.

"My contract isn't going to be renewed," he blurted, not knowing why he was telling her this, why he was admitting this to a woman he'd only just met. "My career is likely over at the end of this season."

Her eyes widened, mouth dropping open for a couple of seconds. Then she shrugged. "Look, I'm sorry. That sucks, but also . . . I'm not really sure what that has to do with me. With *you* putting your hands on me. I'm—" She sighed, shook her head. "Just go, Liam."

Then she turned and disappeared into the bathroom, closing —and locking, the *click* of the mechanism loud in the quiet studio —the door behind her.

When she didn't come out for long moments, he left.

He'd overstepped. He'd put his hands on her.

He'd been a weird guy hijacking her place of business.

And . . . she'd laid him flat.

In more ways than one.

Sighing, he made his way across the crosswalk without almost getting mowed over this time, started to get into his car, but paused when he saw the parking ticket on the windshield.

"Cool, universe, thanks for that," he grumbled, grabbing it and dropping himself into the driver's seat.

But instead of driving off, he waited.

Waited until the lights flicked off inside the karate studio. Waited until Mia came out. Waited until she locked the door behind her. Waited—

Until she unerringly met his gaze across the street, through the window of his car. She held his stare for a long moment then nodded, striding confidently down the sidewalk in a loose sweatshirt and leggings.

It was dark. She shouldn't be able to see him.

But she had.

And maybe *that* was the truest statement he'd ever thought about his life.

Four

MIA

Guilt wasn't a nice feeling.
But Mia didn't do nice.
Ever.

So maybe guilt fit right in. She certainly had shouldered her fair share of it over the years.

She lay awake, eyes on the ceiling, already having gone through her tried and true techniques for sleep—quieting her mind by going over the next day's lesson plan, reviewing the forms she taught her students, the precise combinations of kicks, blocks, and punches came in varying degrees of difficulty based on their level, even counting backward from one hundred—but nothing helped.

Her gaze stayed on the ceiling, her brain was still alert.

Sighing, she pushed out of bed, fingers running over the smoothed edge of the large abalone shell that sat on her nightstand as she went. It was the single bit of clutter in her apartment, but it remained next to her bed, nonetheless. A bed she should be sleeping in, but since she wasn't, Mia knew it was a pointless endeavor to stay under the covers, counting the minutes until the sun rose. Instead, she padded on bare feet through the apartment that was above the studio, the one she'd purposefully circled the block and entered through the back door instead of the interior one when she realized that Liam was going to sit all night in his car watching the place until he saw her leave.

That probably should have made her instincts prickle uncomfortably, or even to piss her off that the man, the stranger who'd dared put hands on her thought he could out-wait her.

But . . . he seemed lost.

That was her first and most overwhelming thought.

Liam seemed like he had a good core, had been helpful, and was apparently also protective, making sure she got out of the studio okay.

He didn't know that there was a staircase hidden behind a door in her office, that she lived above, and while he was giving her instincts definite good-person vibes, she also hadn't wanted him to know where she lived.

She'd spent too long guarding that secret, guarding *all* her secrets.

Sighing, she turned on the shower, letting the water begin to warm up and thankful that she'd invested in a tankless system for the building a couple of months ago after another in a long line of too many cold showers. Still, it took a few minutes to get hot, so she used her time wisely, brewing a pot of coffee, pulling out what would become her breakfast—a whole wheat bagel, peanut butter, and a banana.

By the time she had laid everything on the counter, the water was warm, so she made her way back into the bathroom, stripped down, and showered.

Wash hair. Wash body. Wash face.

Efficient, graceful movements that didn't waste water or time.

Nothing extra. No fluff. No girlie fragranced soap or perfumed shampoo. No soft towels or floral-scented wall plug-ins that filled her apartment with the scent of something fanciful and sweet.

There wasn't room in her life for anything superfluous.

Scents. Men.

They were one in the same to her.

Extra. Meaningless. Of no use.

Or at least, that was what her father had tried to engrain in her.

It had worked for the most part, too, she knew. Aside from a warm shower every morning, she didn't long for much, was content with her small apartment, her students, her hot water.

She finished washing her face then immediately turned off the water, another expectation entrenched in her by her father, and reached for the plain white towel. They were the same towels she and her father had since after her mother had passed. Thin now, needing replacing, but she still knew that when she bought another set, they wouldn't be something fluffy and soft and pink.

They would be utilitarian. Steadfast. Efficient.

Just like her.

She slipped on clean underwear, a bra, sweats, and a T-shirt. Moved back to the kitchen to toast her bagel, to get her mix of grains, protein, and fruit. A well-rounded meal to start the day, even though it was—her eyes flicked to the clock—just after three in the morning.

The building housing her apartment and the studio was old. There was always something that needed repair or replacing, though she tended to rely less on duct tape, super glue, and white paint than her old man, and more on YouTube tutorials and proper supplies from the hardware store.

Plenty of elbow grease was required in both instances, however.

And speaking of elbow grease, Mia washed her dishes, set them on the drying rack, and slipped out the front door of her apartment, down the stairs, and into the studio.

She had lived her whole life above the space, knew exactly where to step, how to avoid any obstacles and not trip over anything as she made her way over to the light switch and flicked it on. Then she spent the next few hours doing her least favorite thing in the world . . . disinfecting the foam squares that snapped together to make up the floor.

Clean one side, pull it up, flip it over, sweep beneath, then clean the other. It didn't take long in the grand scheme of things, less than five minutes per square, but . . . there were a lot of squares.

And so the sun was firmly up by the time she finished.

She glanced over the nearly-sparkling floor for a long moment, thinking about all the times she'd done this before.

Too many to count.

Too many to remember.

Too many times in front of her.

Not liking the sudden tightness that rushed into her at the last thought, Mia tucked the bottle of cleaner away and washed her hands. Then she found her way back out onto the floor, to the X marked with a small strip of tape in the center of the mats, to the spot she'd stood at so often over the years.

Front and center and with plenty of room to move.

This was her favorite place to stand, the spot she always took when they weren't lined up by rank or when she had to present herself to the judges during a testing ceremony or . . . when she had to present herself to her father.

For his tests. His approval. His—

How was it that he had been gone for five years?

It seemed like yesterday he was standing in front of her, the center judge in a group of others who were testing her on her knowledge and abilities in order to decide if she was worthy of that fifth degree.

Five years of training solely for her current rank, having had to wait that long after gaining her fourth degree, protocol demanding she take the time to train, to focus, to put in the years of effort in order to prove herself worthy of the fifth yellow stripe embroidered into her black belt.

Her father had lived to see her pass that test.

But he had only lived six months beyond it.

She sank onto the mat, her body automatically dropping into the warm-up routine she did in her classes, push-ups and sit-ups, planks, and mountain climbers, feeling her heart begin to beat faster, her body temperature to rise.

When her muscles were loose enough, she stood, stretched for a few moments.

And then she began to *move*.

There were a number of forms she had to know, both to teach to her students and for her own work toward her sixth degree. She still had at least a year before she'd be ready to test for it, but the sheer volume of knowledge she needed to be able to present at a moment's notice meant that regular practice was required.

But not only that, the open form she'd been required to prepare—basically she got to make up her own combination of moves as one part of the test—was one of her favorite forms she'd ever done.

Mia had been able to do all her favorite things, play to her strengths, focus on her flexibility, her grace, her ability to transition smoothly from one move to the next.

Inhaling deeply, then releasing her breath slowly, she took one moment to focus.

Then she began to run through that beloved form.

Slow. Slow. Quick. A jumping, spinning kick moving rapidly toward the mirrors, but a quiet landing. Then transiting to the other direction, blocking, pretending she was battling multiple attackers.

Turn. A flurry of kicks, of blocks that were interspersed with control. Long, slow movements designed to show off her balance.

Sweat began to bead on her forehead, slide down her back.

Her breath came quickly, the sound of it mixing with the soft pad of her feet on the mat as she landed, shifted, punched, and kicked fiercely in the quiet space.

A few moves from the end though, her arms began to burn, her legs struggled to launch her into the air for one more jumping-spin-hook kick. But that was part of the beauty of it, part of the beauty of this sport. Pushing through, persevering. Strength, courage, grace.

She landed on the balls of her feet, completed the final flurry of punches, and then turned, stepping into the final stance, holding it for a long moment.

During the test, the judges could ask her to hold that final move for as long as they wanted.

But today she stayed in place until her pulse calmed, her breathing evened out.

That was when she felt the prickling on her nape.

Her eyes flashed up to the mirror in front of her, and her heart picked up its pace again when she saw who was staring at her through the plate glass window.

She'd raised the shades an hour before, letting the sunshine in.

But she'd also let Liam in. Or rather, to *glimpse* in. Tall, dark, and handsome stood on the sidewalk outside the studio, his face a blank shell, a white bag clutched in one hand, a tray with coffee cups in the other.

Her breath caught, suddenly as out of breath as she had been at the end of her form, and she spun. His face transformed from blank to amazing, and Mia watched as his lips formed the word, "Wow." Not gonna lie, that made a curl of pleasure coil in her stomach. She was used to people watching her, spent most of her time on display, but not exactly like *this*.

A man with heat in his expression, his eyes slowly sweeping down her body and then back up.

That long, inching perusal set fire to the veins of a woman who didn't deal in extras and fluff, but rather who dealt in reality, in black and white, right and wrong, A led to B.

Her body liked the fluff of that long, slow look.

It wondered why A couldn't lead to . . . fucking.

The last thought pulled her back into herself, her mind to sharp focus. A virtual stranger was outside her door. That was creepy and pushing the boundaries, no matter that her body liked the look of his. Further, it had been a good three months since she'd been on a date, and maybe three—no, *four* months before that since she'd been on the receiving end of an orgasm that wasn't courtesy of her and her vibrator.

She was pent up.

That was why she was so attracted to the first halfway decent, single man who'd showed her the least bit of attention.

Or . . . she thought he was single.

That hadn't really been made clear.

The knock on the door made her eyes—which had been staring at the glass but not really taking in Liam because her mind was too lost in thought—focus on the man outside. He held up the coffee and bag, mouthed, "Hungry?"

She wasn't.

She *was*.

But this was fluff. The attraction. The man waiting for her to make it safely out of the studio the night before. The fact that he'd brought breakfast now.

And it went against everything inside her to move toward that fluff.

"Fuck," she muttered, annoyed with herself, her thoughts, her indecisions. This wasn't her. Mia was a straight arrow, the straightest fucking arrow on the planet. She didn't waver, and she sure as hell didn't worry about fluff. "Enough goddamned fluff," she growled, striding toward the door and glaring out at Liam. "What are you doing here?" she snapped through the glass.

He put a hand to his ear. "What?"

"What are you doing *here?*" she asked louder.

His hand stayed up, cupping his ear. "*What?*"

Later, she would realize that both of his *whats* were crystal clear to her ears, which also meant that her questions had to be perfectly audible to his. But she'd been up for several hours already, was sweaty and a little shaky from her form—and *only* her form, because she didn't give one damn about the fact that this man was just on the other side of the glass (. . . and *no* she wasn't going to examine that thought too closely because she was living in glorious delusion at the moment).

So, it was certainly either the fatigue or brain fog (and *not* the man), that had her sighing and reaching over to unlatch the lock.

Liam grabbed the handle, quickly opening the door, probably assuming—rightly, she could admit—that she'd regretted the move and wanted to lock it just as rapidly. But then it was unlocked, it was open, and . . . he was inside, mere inches from her.

"Morning," he said softly, his voice a little husky and way too sexy for her comfort.

She shivered, stepped back before she caught herself. Dammit, she was a Caldwell. They didn't retreat. They pressed forward. They bided their time before they struck—

"Why do you look like you want to punch me?" he asked, still soft, though there was a glimmer of mischief in those stormy gray eyes.

"Probably because I do," she told him, crossing her arms.

Instead of backing off or leaving, like she half-expected him to do—she *had* put him on his ass twice the day before after all, so he'd be stupid not to tread a *little* cautiously—he stayed in place, studying her closely. "You're tired," he said.

Something unfurled inside her and she frowned, both at the words and the strange sensation pulsing through her.

Not desire—*that* seemed to be at a baseline level that made her skin prickle, her pussy throb, her breasts feel heavy and aching when within eyesight of this man.

It was . . . soft.

Fluff.

Uh-oh.

FIVE

LIAM

He watched Mia's face gentle for the barest second, but then gentle was gone, her pretty brown eyes narrowed, and her lips pressed flat.

"I was working out," she muttered. "Of course I look tired."

"No," he found himself saying, probably stupidly because he hardly knew Mia from Eve. But . . . there was something deeply tired about her this morning, as though the weight of the world was on her shoulders.

He hadn't seen it last night.

She'd been impenetrable.

But in the light of the early morning, his protective instincts flared.

"*No?*" she asked with raised brows.

"No," he repeated, stepping closer. "You're not physically tired. It's . . . you're tired"—he tapped his chest, the spot just above his heart—"here."

Mia shook her head. "What are you trying to do, Liam?" she asked. "Be the female whisperer? Or maybe, you're that hard up from a lack of puck bunnies that you're going after a normal woman like me?"

"You're not normal."

Outrage flittered across her face, and it wasn't like he could blame her, because—shit—that had come out sounding a lot worse than he'd intended.

"That's not—" he began.

Her face blanked out, going completely devoid of emotion. "Is one of those for me?" She nodded at the coffee.

He floundered for a second, trying to decide if it would piss her off more to keep going with his explanation, to try and clarify what he'd meant with the whole *not normal* thing, or to just ply her with caffeine. "Yes," Liam said, nodding at the cup in front, "caramel macchiato"—then to the one at the back—"white chocolate mocha."

She went still, whispered something that sounded like, "Fluff." But before he could ask her what she'd said or what *fluff* meant, if he'd even heard that right, Mia lifted her chin and said, "And the bag?"

"Bagel sandwiches."

Her eyes flared. "Why?"

"Why what?"

"Why did you bring that stuff?"

Um. Wasn't that obvious? He thought she was capable and gorgeous and strong and—

"You're a puzzle," he blurted instead of any of those "normal" things. Fuck.

Her head tilted to the side, long black hair swinging behind her in a shining tail, brows drawn together as she scoffed. "You're insane."

"Because I think you're a puzzle?"

"I'm the most straightforward person you'll ever meet."

His lips ghosted up into a smile. "That's probably true," he agreed. "But I'm not talking about what's on the surface."

She rolled her eyes.

"You're a puzzle," Liam repeated, setting the tray of coffee down on the small table by the door, stashing the bag alongside it. He stepped closer, not near enough to touch, because he'd learned his lesson, but within proximity to see clearly that those brown eyes hid a little green. More secrets hidden beneath the surface. "Because on the outside," he said, "you seem to be only hard edges and barbed wire, but there's something . . . delicate inside you."

That wasn't exactly the word he wanted to use, but he didn't think Mia would like it if he substituted with the one he was really thinking—that being, fragile.

Because there was something breakable and delicate about this woman.

Crystal covered in steel.

Get through the top layers in order to see the beauty beneath.

"Delicate?" she asked with an arched brow.

"That's no comment on your ass-kicking skills, J.B.," he said, lips tipped up, fingers brushing lightly over the bruise on his jaw that had emerged in all its purple-and-black glory from her elbow the night before. "You've demonstrated them quite efficiently."

She narrowed her eyes. "Don't call me baby."

"J.B.," he said quickly. "Like the letters. Not *baby*."

Her eyes remained narrowed, brow lifted. "What the hell does that mean?"

He decided his best course of action was a distraction and picked up the coffees again. "Macchiato or mocha?"

"Do you know how much sugar is in those?" she said, still not relaxing, that eyebrow still raised.

It probably hinted at his fucked-up-ness that he enjoyed that brow, was amused by the sharp tone. But he'd never been attracted to weak women. His mom was "all brass balls and steel wool"—that was a direct quote from his dad, and although his parents had never shared the hidden meaning behind it, Liam had heard the phrase so much over the years that he knew he'd never be able to think of a more perfect description.

She'd had to be strong and a little abrasive to deal with three boys, all only two years apart, and a professional hockey player husband who traveled for half the season.

She'd had to have giant proverbial balls to deal with his grandfather.

Hank Williamson, who had also been a professional hockey player, who was very much of the "men bring home the bacon, the women have kids" sect.

Well, that wasn't Liam's mom. Not one iota.

Fran had wanted a family—though Liam wasn't sure if three boys under the age of six had been her plan. But regardless, he and his brothers had been born close together, and though she'd been involved at their schools and during sports, she'd also been a high-powered executive at a local bank.

Not a pushover.

Strong and capable . . . like the woman in front of him.

"I think after that routine," he told her, shoving the mocha in her direction since it was the less sweet of the two drinks, "you deserve a little sugar." He let go when he'd perched it on her still crossed arms and she sighed, shifted carefully to grab it. "Let me guess, you take your coffee black?"

She rolled her eyes but didn't answer him.

"You do," he said. "Is that what makes you jump so high?"

A snort. "I just prefer it black, okay?"

"Are you a vegetarian?"

Her head tilted to the side, probably at the sharp right turn in conversation. "No."

"A vegan?"

Another head tilt, this time in the other direction. It was as cute as the tiny furrow between her brows. "No," she said again.

Liam grinned inwardly, thinking that Mia would appreciate being called cute in any fashion about as much as she'd appreciated him referring to her as delicate. Tempted as he was to say it aloud, just to see her reaction, he figured he'd pushed her far enough for the moment, so he spun, retrieved the bag of bagels, and sat down on one of the chairs by the door, opening the folded top and pulling out the two sandwiches. "Bacon or sausage?" he asked.

She frowned, that tiny furrow growing larger.

"Bacon, it is," he said, pulling the paper-wrapped sandwich out and waving it in her direction.

The delicious smell of meat filled the space. Meat. *Heh*. Liam had to bite back a snort. The guys on the Gold had corrupted him. He used to be a mature twenty-five-year-old man who'd had a normal sense of humor. A couple weeks with the team, and he'd regressed about fourteen years.

"Come on," he said, focusing on the gorgeous woman in front of him instead of the middle school humor. "It's my cheat day, don't let it go to waste." He grinned. "Or worse, don't leave it around for me to eat. I'll feel like shit tomorrow."

Silence.

Stiff shoulders, an undrunk cup of coffee in her hand.

He set the sandwich on the chair next to him, pulled out the sausage one—also, *heh*—and began eating. "Oh my God," he mumbled through the sandwich. "This is amazing." He took another bite, rubbed his stomach. "It might be the best bagel I've ever had."

Mia rolled her eyes.

He chewed, swallowed, then took another bite. "Oh my—"

"Is that sandwich going to make you come, too?"

Liam inhaled and immediately started choking on the giant bite he'd shoved into his mouth, and apparently being near death was the one thing that would drive Mia off her spot on the mat.

She crossed over to him, took the bagel from his hands and set it down on the chair, then knelt in front of him, ordered, "Lift your arms up."

He glanced at her, confused at what his arms had to with the fact that he was coughing like hell. Mia made an annoyed noise, leaned close, and grabbed his wrists, yanking his arms over his head.

Immediately, his lungs eased, the urge to cough lessened, and he was finally able to suck in a deep breath.

"How?" he asked when he was finally able to talk.

She shrugged, making his nerves stand at rigid attention when he realized how close she was. Her arms were pressed to his. Her chest mere inches away. Her mouth—

Close enough to feel her hot breath.

"It doesn't work if you're really choking," she said. "But it helps get a bit more oxygen into your lungs if you're not, often relaxes the diaphragm enough for someone to regain their breath."

"And if a person was really choking?" he asked.

The hint of a smile. "Heimlich is our friend." She released his wrists but didn't back away, and Liam found himself lowering his arms inch by careful inch in order to not scare her into putting some distance between them.

"Thank you," he murmured, once his palms were on his knees.

Another shrug, head tilting to the side again. "What did you mean by Cheat Day?"

He chuckled. "The Gold have a very strict diet plan for the season. No dairy, no sugar, no meat for the most part, no processed foods, no extra carbs or sodium, no trans fats—"

"Is there anything you *can* eat?" she asked, and the humor warming those striking brown eyes had him clenching his knees in order to not reach out and tug her close, to see if she would taste like the interesting combination of sweet and tart that was her personality.

"Plant-based protein. Water—" He broke off on a laugh at her expression.

"First, water is drinking not eating," she said. "Second, plant-based protein?" Her eyes cut to the bagel in his hands, the sausage patty clearly evident.

"As I said, Cheat Day," he told her. "Our nutritionist is strict, but she is also realistic."

"So bagels and coffee?" she asked, shifting back and standing. "That's your Cheat Day?"

"Live vicariously with me." He picked up his breakfast sandwich then hers, holding it up to her.

Her eyes went to his, held.

Then she sighed, grabbing the bagel and sitting down. She left two empty chairs between them, and he knew it was as deliberate a gesture as was Nutritionist Rebecca's meal plan. That being, exceptionally so.

"This is you living vicariously?" she asked, glancing back and forth between the bagel and his face, expression incredulous.

"I'm a simple man."

She snorted, rolled her eyes as she opened the wrapper. "I don't think there's anything simple about you."

"Is this a case of takes one to know one?"

At his question, Mia froze and then she laughed—a tinkling sound filled with such humor, and he stared at her, wanting to capture it in his memory. He didn't know what he'd said, but if it made her laugh like that, he'd do it again and again and *again*.

"I am the most boring person on the planet," she said. "I've lived in San Francisco my whole life, in the same apartment. I've even had the same haircut—just a trim every six weeks—since I was a little girl. My dad—" She cut herself off on a sigh. "Why am I telling you this?"

"Because we have a connection," he said, taking some of her tact and being blunt.

Her gaze flew to his, away. "You just think that because I stopped you from turning into a San Franciscan pancake."

Liam grinned. "Maybe." His voice gentled. "But I think it's something else, too."

A shake of her head. "No."

Panic edged into the lines of her face, and he took a mental step back. He might not have been able to sleep the night before, he was so fascinated by the puzzle that Mia presented, but he was also . . . the invader here.

And if he'd learned anything about this woman from the night before, from watching her run through the routine of kicks and punches on the floor, it was that she didn't like surprises, that she preferred everything run exactly as planned. Her life had structure and expectations . . .

Not a virtual stranger showing up at her door twice in as many days.

And yet—

Liam hadn't been able to stay away.

Patience, he counseled himself. *Slow and steady and see if she turns out to be the fascinating creature you think she'll be.*

Creature?

Wow. He was bringing the romance and charm that morning. Good thing he'd kept that thought where it belonged—in his mind.

He nudged the sandwich toward her mouth. "I promise it's not drugged."

Mia scowled. "And is that why you keep pressuring me to eat it?"

"Fine." He snatched it from her, took a large bite and groaned in pleasure. "If you won't eat it, I will."

"Rude," she snapped, snatching it from him. "That's mine." She bit off a mouthful and immediately moaned, the sound going straight to his cock. "This is delicious."

"I know." He took another bite from his bagel, more to shut himself up than because he could really taste the food. What he wouldn't give to hear her make that noise again, preferably when they were both naked.

They ate quietly for the next while, the silence only broken by his laughter when Mia took a drink of her coffee, winced, and immediately set it aside.

"Not for you?" Liam asked.

"That's like eating a straight spoonful of sugar." She got up, went to the water fountain on the side of the studio and took a long sip. "How can you drink that crap?"

He shrugged. "What can I say? I have a sweet tooth."

She sniffed, walked back over, picked up the cup and handed it to him. "Well, *I* can say thanks for bringing it, but enjoy this addition to your Cheat Day."

Shoving the last bite of bagel into his mouth, he reached for the cup she held out.

"Not going to protest?" she asked.

A shake of his head. "Absolutely not. I'll take my sugar any way I can get it, especially on Cheat Days."

"Oh boy."

Liam took a sip from the mocha, which was his preferred coffee. He'd only gotten the macchiato in the first place because it was their starting goalie's favorite drink, and she was pretty much the only female he'd gotten to know semi-well over the last few years.

He didn't date much, and he'd been traveling or traded to different teams so often since he'd made the transition to the NHL that it was hard to grow roots.

Hell, he'd been shuffled between three teams in the course of twenty-four hours before the Gold had picked him up at the trade deadline. Liam pushed away the memory of how embarrassing it had been to be a Williamson who was so clearly on the leeward side of his career. Even until they'd retired, his brothers and father had been sought after. They'd made sure to go out on top.

But they'd also been successful from almost the beginning.

Exploding out in their rookie seasons, being valuable additions to their teams, leaders that helped their respective organizations win the Cup.

Basically, they hadn't struggled. Unlike him.

"Not going to drink that one, too?" Mia asked.

He shook his head, more to clear the negative thoughts than in answer. "No, I have practice tomorrow and a game the day after," he said. "I might joke about my sweet tooth and sugar-inhaling abilities, but I don't want to go too crazy and feel like shit on the ice."

"Hmm."

"What?"

That *hmm* had been decidedly pleased, but she merely shook her head in answer.

"Plus," he said, "Nutritionist Rebecca's food plan is legit. I don't think I've had this much energy . . . ever."

"*Nutritionist* Rebecca?"

He shrugged. "Not so funny story, we have two Rebeccas in the organization. They've titled themselves."

Mia's lips twitched. "And what's the other Rebecca?"

"PR Rebecca."

"The nicknames don't exactly flow off the tongue now, do they?"

"No." He laughed lightly. "Can't say it does."

She polished off the rest of her bagel, crumpled the wrapper, and took his and the empty bag to the trash then surprised him by not kicking his sorry ass out the door and instead sitting back down next to him, albeit still with the two empty chairs between them. Her eyes locked onto his. "Why are we here, Liam?"

"Here in a proverbial sense?"

A roll of those warm brown irises.

"Ah," he said lightly. "Why in the literal sense then."

"Liam," she warned.

"I wanted to apologize, okay?"

Her stare hardened. "So, you did that by showing up at eight in the morning at my place of business?"

Round and round in circles in his mind. Round and round in this conversation with this woman. What to say? What to hide? How to explain? How not to scare her off? He didn't have any great answers to any of it. All he knew was—

"I like you, okay?"

So not smooth.

Would probably scare her off anyway.

Would *certainly* have his ass bustled to the door.

Except . . . she *didn't* bustle him to the door. Instead, she remained sitting two chairs over from him, mouth agape, and went mute.

Totally, utterly mute.

"What?" he finally asked.

She blinked. "You."

"Me, what?"

She exploded to her feet. "You can't like *me!*" Her steps were quiet as she paced away. "You hardly know me. Y-you—"

He stood and crossed over to her.

Not touching, because she'd drawn that boundary, but near enough to catch a whiff of soap, the slight spice of exertion from her exercise.

"You saved my life," he said. "I think that's a good place to start."

"So, this is some sort of Stockholm Syndrome?"

"Well, no, because you didn't kidnap me." He reached a hand out, wanting to lightly tug the end of her ponytail, to pair the teasing with touch, but then he remembered the whole no-permission-to-touch thing and pulled back. Which meant he looked like some sort of strange lobster puppet creature, reaching out thumb and forefinger, pulling back and shifting back to his heels.

Her lips pressed flat, not seeming to notice, or maybe it was less that and more not acknowledging his weirdness. Either way, she just stayed in place. "Right." A scowl. "That's for kidnapping. I wonder what the term for falling for your rescuer is." She tapped her chin, turned away. "There's got to be *something.*"

Liam was frozen in place, struck by the lean lines of her legs encased in her sweats, the shining hair tugged into the ponytail, its end just caressing the top of her ass.

He wanted to touch that hair.

He wanted to touch *her.*

To demonstrate exactly why he could like her, why he'd dreamed about her, why he'd gotten up on a rare day he'd been able to sleep in, and why he'd been thrilled to see her cleaning through the window.

Hint. It was the same reason he'd forced himself to keep walking, to go down the block and pick up food and coffee.

Also, why he'd come back and then been stunned into stillness by the way she moved across the floor. Graceful as a dancer, liquid as water, strong as a check coming right for him.

He'd lifted his hand without realizing it, his fingers less than an inch from her hair.

Coming back into himself, he jumped back.

Of course, Mia caught the movement in the mirror.

She spun, plunked her hands onto her hips. "What the hell are you doing?"

"I—" He shook himself. "You said no touching. I'm trying to abide by that."

Her mouth fell open.

"I-I mean, that sounds stupid, but yesterday you set the boundary. I pushed it, and I shouldn't have." He thrust a hand through his hair and spun away, knowing he sounded like an idiot and was blowing his chance with her. "You were uncomfortable, and it was inappropriate, and even though I'm wildly attracted to you and think you're the coolest person I've met in a long time, I won't cross that line." A sigh as he clenched his hands into fists. "I won't betray the trust you've given me this morning by letting me into your studio."

Silence.

Long enough that he'd actually taken a step toward the door, knowing it was time to show himself out.

This was . . . too much for a day's interaction.

That was the fucking understatement of the year.

"Liam."

He rotated to face her.

"I'm not what you think," she said. Not gentle, not soft. Just clear and concise, as though she were trying to convince both herself *and* him. "I can't be what you think."

"I think you can."

"No," she said, more firmly. "I *can't*."

Fuck. He *had* blown it. "I'll go." Regroup. Come back when—

Gentle fingers on his jaw, a firm hand on his shoulder, turning him to face her.

A lithely muscled female body pressed to his.

"I'm not any of those things you said. I'm not cool or special or exceptional. I'm just . . . Mia."

He was barely breathing, had to force out the words. "Just Mia seems pretty great."

A shake of her head that ponytail swinging again. "Appearances can be deceiving."

He covered her hand with his own, wanted to say something to convince her she was wrong. Instead, he ended up saying the only thing he could think, "Your skin is like silk."

She shivered. "Yours is scalding hot."

"Let me take you out to dinner."

A statue in his arms, flush against him. "I'm not sure that's a good idea."

"What can I do to convince you?"

Those brown eyes flared with heat, speared him in place, a shuddering breath sliding between her lips. Statue no more, her body softened, breast brushing his chest, thighs tangling with his. A red haze appeared in the corners of his vision.

Then she rose on tiptoe. "Come home with me."

That red haze spread . . . and consumed him alive.

Six

MIA

The words were hardly out of her mouth before panic slipped in.

What was she doing? Dear God, what in the *fuck* was she doing?

She didn't invite men upstairs, certainly didn't sleep with men she didn't know.

But then again, she also didn't let strange men into her studio in the early morning, didn't eat food they'd brought, or drink the sugary coffee. Well, she didn't have men showing up bearing gifts, either.

She also didn't have men look at her the way that Liam did.

And . . . she found she didn't want it to stop.

Like it inevitably would if she went out to dinner with him.

If she could just capture this moment, bottle it and tuck it on a shelf for safekeeping, if she could just pretend for one day, one hour that this man might actually like her when he came to know her, that he wouldn't mind the lack of fluff, the sharp edges and occasional sharp tone—

Then what?

She'd be worthy?

A sick, black feeling crept down her spine.

His palm slid from covering her hand, across the outside of her wrist, up her forearm, slowly crawling over her skin until he cupped her cheek. "I would in a second," he said, "but I don't think that's what you really want."

It was instinct to break away.

"You should go," she said, eyes on the mat, back to him. "You should just go, now." Before he got to know her. Before he was disappointed by her. Before he found out—

A pause. Then, "Before I find out what?"

Mia whirled around, horror coursing through her. She hadn't said the last part of her thinking aloud, she hadn't.

She. Hadn't.

His eyes didn't hold revulsion and that more than anything, told her she hadn't said it, hadn't hinted at the truth that continued to eat her alive. And yet this man knew she was hiding something. Knew she was running from the pain of her past.

Because she might not have fluff, but she sure as shit had secrets.

Painful secrets that had honed her to a sharp, cutting edge.

"I know this is crazy," he said, voice careful. "I know we're strangers and I shouldn't care what's going on in your head. I know you think my interest is because you helped me or because I'm some creep who needs to get laid." He took a step toward her, stopped when her breath caught audibly. "But it's not that."

She didn't move, though her pulse was pounding in her veins. "What then?"

"I looked into your eyes, and I saw . . ."

Her lungs froze. Her mouth went dry.

Mia waited for him to finish the trailed off sentence, waited an eternity it seemed before he inhaled and said, "I looked into your eyes, and I saw . . . me."

She frowned.

"I know," he said, volume dropping, almost as if he was

talking to himself. "It makes no sense. This sounds like something out of a bad romcom movie, and plus, who knows how long I'll even be in California? My contract probably won't be renewed. I'll just be some unemployed nobody who—" Liam physically shook himself. "Yeah, so that's it. I saw you, felt like some part of me knew some part of you—" He cut himself off with a derisive snort. "Know what? I'm just going to stop there."

Her throat had closed up, stifling any words that might come out.

She'd felt it, too.

She felt it *now*.

Drawn to this man in a way that made no sense. A way that made her want to forget everything she'd learned about herself up to this point, to throw caution to the wind. But . . .

She couldn't.

He might like her now and be drawn to her, but sooner or later he'd see what was inside her, and he'd—

"I'll go," he said, turning for the door.

Slice.

That movement cut through her, pierced right through the protective coating surrounding her, and Mia found words coming out of her mouth before she rationally processed them.

"Don't," she said. "Don't go."

He stopped, turned to face her, and those words that had blurted out so freely disappeared on her, nothing further coming out. Instead, she just stood there like a mute robot, unable to push anything else from between her lips.

An itchy, unbearable agony began to fill her.

Say something! This was her job—to have the words, to give directions. Instead, she was just staring at him like a puppet who'd lost her master and was reduced to a limp pile of fabric and strings.

"Want to take a walk?"

His question made the itchy feeling fade, the stifling blackness that was making it impossible for her to form words disappear.

She considered him for a second, thought of what she might do if he left or if she told him no and returned to the apartment. Everything would stay the same. Nothing would change. And she'd miss out . . . on what?

That she wasn't sure of.

All she knew was that she didn't want to.

Mia bit the inside of her cheek then sucked in a slow, even breath. A heartbeat later, she went with her instincts and said, "Okay."

"Okay." He smiled, the visceral impact of that a punch to the gut, before he grabbed the remaining coffee cup, and moved to the door, holding it open. Mia took a step toward him, felt a gust of cold morning air, so she veered off and made a pit stop at her office, snagging the sweatshirt she always kept there, along with the spare front door key, and slipped the sweatshirt over her head.

"Good?" he asked when she'd crossed back over to him.

She nodded.

He waved a hand forward, indicating she should precede him through the door. But when she did, she felt his fingers on her nape, tugging free the end of her ponytail that was trapped beneath the collar of her sweatshirt.

"Okay?" he asked, voice soft, sticking to the one-word questions, which, honestly, was preferred for her psyche at the moment. Heat had exploded through her from the simple contact, the light brush of his fingers along the back of her neck making her shiver, and she found she could barely process the word, let alone form words.

Instead, she merely nodded again, let him hold the door for her, and moved out onto the sidewalk.

He stepped out, too, and released the handle, waiting as she locked up. After she had, she glanced at his handsome face, saw the bruise on his jaw, still forming. It was already black and blue and would be all sorts of shades of purple before the day was out.

"I'm sorry I hurt you." Liam's gaze met hers, and guilt tore through her. "Last night. I—"

She shouldn't have hit him.

"Don't ever apologize for protecting yourself." His fingers trailed lightly down her arm, a smile teasing the corners of his mouth. "I had it coming."

She bit her lip. "Maybe."

That smile went grin and he tilted his head forward, started walking . . . and as she fell into step beside him, she started thinking again. Why was she going off with a man she didn't know? She'd yell at her students for even considering the idea.

But then Liam took her hand.

The thoughts quieted.

The sharp edges were smoothed out.

And . . . she walked.

———

"We absolutely cannot be here," Mia said.

"Why not?"

"Why *not?*" She stamped her foot. Yes, literally stamped her foot on the cracked sidewalk. "*Why not?*"

Liam still held her hand, their fingers interlaced as they had been for the entire time they'd walked. At first, she'd thought they were just wandering, but then she realized he was leading her to a specific destination, up through the residential area that abutted the studio, winding through the houses and apartments until he'd led her to a small park.

She'd been to this park before.

Many times.

Of course she had. It was within walking distance of the karate studio, and there wasn't a lot of green space in the city, though this neighborhood, with houses that actually had back-yards and several other parks dotting the area, perhaps had more green space than many places in San Francisco.

"Yes," he said, tugging her hand, leading her up the curved incline that led to the top of the hill. "Why can't we be here?"

She yanked her hand from his, used it to point to the green sign directly behind him. "That!" she snapped. "That says right there why."

He turned, read aloud the second rule. "No adults unless accompanied by children." A beat. "Hmm." Then he shrugged, moved toward the top of the slide that this park was known for. Well, technically it was a pair of steep concrete slides.

"We don't have kids."

Another shrug. "But you work with kids," he said. "That has to count for something."

"Liam—" She didn't know what to say to that.

His eyes flicked back to the sign.

"*And* it's Tuesday." He tsked, pointing to the part of the sign she'd missed—the fact that it was only open Wednesday through Sunday from ten in the morning until five at night. "And"—a glance down at his watch—"it's not even ten o'clock." Humor filled those gray eyes. "We're breaking *all* the rules today."

"I—" She took a step back. "Liam—" Mia waved a hand at the slide itself, where a metal gate was installed at the top and wouldn't be opened until ten the next day. "Look, we can't even do this anyway. Everything is locked up, and we don't have any cardboard."

He frowned. "Why would we need cardboard?"

"You slide down on it, and it makes you go faster."

That earned her a grin. "I like faster."

"I know," she said, adding when she read the question in his gaze, "I saw you move on the ice."

His eyes sparked with humor. "I had figure skating classes when I was young."

She gasped. "No, you didn't." That just did not fit in with her tough, hockey player mental picture.

"I did," he said, wandering over to the side of the slide and glancing down. "It's actually not unheard of. Figure skaters tend to be much more graceful than us big brutes."

"Yeah, I was wondering about that."

"Wondering about what?" he asked, straightening then moving over to glance behind several pots that were grouped together, the community surrounding the park having come together to grow a small, shared garden.

"Aren't you a little short for a hockey player?"

"But not for a stormtrooper." She was frowning, confused at the statement when he bent with an "Ah-ha!" Then stood with several pieces of cardboard in his hand. He turned. "Now, don't tell me that a woman who can nearly kick the ceiling can't climb over one teensy gate."

"That's not the point."

He shoved a piece of cardboard in her direction and when she wouldn't take it, set it at her feet, leaning it against her knee. "What *is* the point?"

"It's against the rules."

"And you don't break the rules?"

"No."

"Not ever?"

She shook her head. "No, Liam. The rules are there for a reason."

He tucked the cardboard under his arm, moved toward the top of the slide. "And if the rules said to throw yourself off a bridge . . ."

Plunking her hands on her hips, Mia snapped, "You're not seriously comparing the opening hours for a park with an order to do self-harm, are you?"

"And if I was?"

He chuckled at her outraged noise, then climbed over the little gate, put the cardboard down, sat on top of it, and . . . disappeared.

His whoop of pleasure warmed something inside her, and she found herself running forward, leaning over the edge in order to watch him fly down the concrete slide. Moments later, he was at the bottom, gathering up the cardboard and loping back up to her side.

"You know you want to," he said, hopping up onto the platform and coming toward her. His energy was infectious, making her yearn for . . .

More.

She bit her bottom lip.

He groaned softly.

"What?" she whispered.

"Promise you won't flip me onto my ass again?"

"I don't make promises I can't keep."

Liam laughed, and the sound of his slightly rasping chuckle, the warmth in his eyes, the way his body bent slightly, coming close enough to hers that she could smell the spicy, masculine scent of him made Mia's head spin.

"I guess I'll have to take my chances." He brushed his knuckles on the outside of her arm. "When you bite your lip like that, I want it to be my teeth doing the biting."

Her breath shuddered out. "Why?"

His thumb traced lightly over the corner of her mouth. "I think you already know the answer to that question." Hot breath coated her lips when he shifted closer. "You have the most kissable mouth I've ever seen, did you know that?"

Pulse pounding, she managed to say, "How could I possibly know that?"

He smiled at the tart rejoinder. "Come on and break the rules with me," he said, stepping back and holding out his hand. "Just this once."

Mia hesitated, studying the face of this man who'd wreaked so much havoc in so little time. "Once," she said and returned to where she'd knocked the piece of cardboard he'd given her to the concrete, bent to snag it. His smile widened, and again it hit her in the solar plexus with all the force of a punch. "Th-that's it," she added, straightening her spine and breathing through the impact. "Just one time."

She'd only ever used the technique in sparring—the breathing through impact, pushing air through her lungs.

But . . . she supposed this was a type of sparring as well.

Which probably shouldn't have made her feel better, even though it did anyway. Grinning, she tucked the cardboard under her arm, bypassed Liam's hand, and slithered her way between the metal horseshoe that topped the slides and the gate that was in place because the park was technically closed.

"Like the way you move, J.B.," came the husky male voice.

"You going to talk?" she asked, even though the compliment secretly pleased her. "Or are you going to actually come over here and slide?"

"Big words for a woman who wasn't going to break the rules a minute ago," he teased.

"Less talk and more action from the man who's apparently ready to break *all* of them," she countered, and got a flash of his sexy grin again . . . then a nice ass—*ha*—view of a very nice ass. Which made her remember something she'd overhead Brayden's stepmom, Angie, say. Unfortunately for Mia, she also murmured those remembered words out loud, "Hockey players have the best asses."

"What was that?" Liam was halfway through the horseshoe and gate, and her words made him tilt forward dangerously, almost lose his grip.

She grabbed his arm. "Careful."

"What did you say?" he asked again.

Yeah, that wasn't going to be uttered aloud—not *ever* again. In fact, Mia figured she was going to take it to her grave, bury it in the coffin with her.

"Nothing," she muttered.

"Mia."

"I said *nothing*," she repeated.

Playful gray eyes, less storm cloud, more tendrils of ocean fog teasing at the ends of her hair.

"I like your ass, too," he whispered huskily.

God, she wanted to kiss this man, to grab hold of his ears and tug his head down and just kiss him until she forgot to breathe.

But she also wanted . . . fluff.

To play. To forget. To do something that didn't necessarily fit in with the rules she'd used to structure her life.

Why?

She wasn't prepared to consider that last one too closely.

So, just as Liam slipped through the gap, she plunked the cardboard down, parked *her* ass down onto it, and pushed off. "Last one down buys lunch!" she called, flying down the concrete, not wholly understanding where the words came from, but knowing that this man unlocked something inside her. Mischief or hell, maybe it was just as simple as yearning to have some fun for a change.

Either way, she was tearing down the slide, her ponytail whipping behind her, the morning air a cool kiss on her lips, her nose, her cheeks.

She was almost to the bottom when she sensed him coming up behind her.

Too fast.

Because she was slowing down.

Instinctively, she leaned forward, trying to gain speed, but physics and gravity were against her.

Liam was heavier, and his weight combined with them carried him farther.

She continued to slow as he slid by her, his feet finding the ground, and he was standing by the time she made it to the bottom. Her legs flew off the end, but before she could rise, he was there, toes of his shoes pressed to hers. He put out a hand. She didn't need the help, but took it anyway, let him tug her up, allowed her body to press against his.

"You owe me lunch," he breathed, his lips a hairsbreadth from hers.

He ran the back of his knuckles lightly over her cheek, and she shivered, heat spearing through her, filling her with such want and need that she half-expected to be reduced to ash.

Instead, she looked down to find she wasn't.

Instead, she looked down to see his hand resting on her hip.

And . . . *God* how she liked seeing it there, wanted it on her breasts, slipping between her thighs, and—

"What just went through your mind?" he asked, turning his hand over, cupping her cheek, the rough pads of his callouses against her skin making her shiver.

Mia didn't answer.

Instead, she gave in.

SEVEN

LIAM

He was contemplating if Mia would let him stroke his hand down to her neck, to touch the glossy black of her hair, to run the strands over his fingers and see if they were as silky soft as he'd been dreaming about.

Then . . . she kissed him.

Electricity.

The contact exploded across his nerve endings, and Liam moved, one arm banding around her waist, pulling her tighter against him, using his tongue to part her lips, to slip inside her mouth and to taste her more completely.

She tasted of mint and sugar. Logic would reason it was the mocha that sweetened her mouth, but he knew it was just Mia. That she was soft and sweet and pure on the inside, even though it was hidden beneath cool steel on the surface.

Her hands tightened in his hair, tongue darting forward to dance with his.

And Liam lost himself.

There was no learning her. There was just . . . *knowing* this woman, somehow instinctively understanding what she liked, as though his mouth had been made to kiss hers.

She moaned when he drew her closer, melted when he nipped her bottom lip, gasped when he tore his mouth away and trailed it along her jaw, her throat.

He let her tug his head back up, pull him toward her for another kiss.

Fire.

The touch of her lips had it exploding within him, holding her tight, kissing her with an intensity that had no business being present on a first date.

That was the thought drawing him back to himself.

Or enough to gentle his hold, his touch, anyway. Enough to remember that though this woman was steel on the outside, she was fragile inside. She needed soft and coaxing. She needed that fluff. She—

Needed air.

Mia tore her mouth away, resting her forehead on his shoulder, the hot puffs of her breath seeping through the cotton of his hoodie, his T-shirt, imprinting themselves onto his skim. He wanted to feel her mouth on his bare skin, to taste her everywhere, to—

Patience.

Gently, he cupped the back of her head, brushing his hand through her ponytail in long, slow caresses, waiting until both their breathing calmed, for him to be able to suck in enough air to speak.

"I think after a kiss like that, I owe *you* lunch."

She froze, went stiff as a board in his arms, and Liam cursed mentally. Fuck. He shouldn't have—

Then her shoulders shuddered in his hold, a soft giggle reaching his ears.

"I think so, too," she said.

As he was reeling from the sound, loving the wave it coiled

inside him, warming him from the inside out, Mia twisted from his embrace, bent to retrieve her cardboard. "Let's go again!"

She ran with cat-like grace up the incline, was slithering between the gate and the bar by the time he got into motion.

Was flying down the concrete as he made his way up.

He stuck his hand out for a high five, was surprised and pleased when she reached over and their palms smacked together as she slid past. He managed to snag her waist as she ran up for another turn, to steal a laughing peck before she escaped, and then they were both sliding down again. Then cajoled another kiss out of her before they headed back up to go another time.

And then they repeated the process again. A slide. A bone-melting kiss. Rinse. Repeat. Again. And again. And—

"Hey!" came a male voice. "You can't be here—"

They'd just landed at the bottom of the slide, cardboard floating to the ground behind them, both their chests heaving from the twin exertions of running up the incline, of them making out at the bottom for several long minutes. Mia's lips, reddened and slightly swollen, were a teasing temptation that continued to draw him in.

But the sound of the man yelling from the top of the slides made them both jump.

And it made panic crowd into her expression.

"The park is closed—"

"Oh my God," she gasped, going pale when he'd much rather see the pink staining her cheeks, from the cool air, from the sliding, from his kisses.

He didn't give her any time to continuing panicking, to keep going pale.

He just snagged her hand and tugged her forward.

She didn't struggle, just ran alongside him, keeping pace with him easily, even though he worked out daily and had a team of trainers to make sure his body was in top shape.

"Oh my God," she said when he'd stopped them several blocks away, pulling them down a quiet street.

The man didn't seem to have pursued them, but Liam had liked her clinging to him way too much to immediately let her go when he'd realized they were safely out of the park. Even now, her back pressed to the brick wall behind her, his body flush against hers, she didn't shy away. Instead, she clutched at his shoulders, breathing fast but not so much that she couldn't talk.

"I'm a criminal," she said. "Oh my God. I'm a criminal—"

He bent his head and kissed her, expecting those fingers to push him away, but the moment his lips touched hers, they gripped tighter, pulled him closer.

"I kind of like you, J.B.," he said, nuzzling into her throat when they broke apart for air. "You're funny."

Quiet.

A *long* stretch of quiet.

"Are you going to tell me the meaning of that nickname?"

Not on her life. "Nope."

She sighed. "You're a bad influence."

"You had fun." He flicked out his tongue, tasted the salt on her skin, felt her rapid pulse. "Admit it."

Recalcitrant silence.

He nipped the spot where her neck met her shoulder. She jumped, one hand sliding up, weaving into his hair.

"Stubborn." A kiss. "Sexy." Another. "Rule-breaker."

Those fingers tightened enough to make him wince. Then just as quickly relaxed. "I'm not . . . buying lunch."

Liam froze then burst out laughing, pushing off her, snagging her hand again.

As they walked down the street, back in the direction of her studio, he checked his phone. "It's just ten now," he said, "a little early for lunch."

"I worked hard doing all those slides," she said. "I'm hungry. If you're not . . ."

"I'm always hungry," he told her, which was true, but also in this situation, mostly about wanting more time with her. He wasn't ready to go back to his condo alone.

"Good." One shoulder lifted then fell in a casual shrug. "Then I guess you're buying me brunch." She tugged him forward. "Come on," she said. "There's a place nearby that I've always wanted to try."

The restaurant was a tiny hole-in-the-wall breakfast joint just around the corner from the karate studio and looked like it had been there a hundred years.

Or maybe just seventy, as it had a decidedly 1950s look.

"You've never eaten here?" he asked, somewhat surprised. "It's so close to your place."

"The way I grew up—" She shook her head. "I don't eat out a lot."

He was more interested in the first sentence and why she'd cut herself off than the second, but before he could press her for more information, the hostess came over and led them to their booth.

Then the waiter was there almost before their asses hit the pleather, efficiently taking their drink orders.

She ordered coffee. Black.

He ordered orange juice and got a raised brow. "It's not technically sweet," he said, once the server had gone.

"It's still full of sugar."

"A man has needs."

Her eyes met his, and his cock twitched at the heat in those chocolate depths. But then Mia's gaze was on the menu, a studious V between her brows, and he forced himself to pick out what he wanted so that he didn't interrupt her perusal.

Plenty of time for an interrogation *after* they ordered.

"What can I get for you folks?" the waiter, a young college-aged male asked, depositing their drinks and pulling out a pad of paper.

"Mia?" Liam said, "you want to go first?"

She smiled at him. "No. I want to see what you order."

"You gonna make fun of me?"

"Probably."

He chuckled, shrugged, and glanced up at the kid. "Orange creamsicle pancakes, please, and a side of bacon, crispy."

Her brows went up, almost to her hairline, then she turned to the waiter and said, "An egg white omelet, please, with peppers, mushrooms, and onions."

"Do you want cheese in that?"

"Hmm." She was quiet for a moment. "Sure, why not? How about Monterey Jack, if you have it?"

"Got it." The waiter made a note. "Whole wheat toast?"

"Perfect. Thank you."

"Of course.

Liam thanked the server again, who then walked away, leaving them alone. "Was ordering cheese in your omelet your idea of really going for it?" he asked, lips twitching.

A pink flush spread over her face, even as she leveled a glare in his direction. "You have no room to talk, Sweet Cheeks."

"Sweet Cheeks?" he said, aghast, though inside he liked this verbal sparring. "A man has *one* vice."

One black brow came up. "Why don't I think it's just *one* vice?"

"I love sugar, okay?" he muttered, not about to admit to anything.

"What else are you obsessed with?" she pressed.

"Tit for tat, here, J.B.," he countered. "You want to know. You have to be prepared to answer *all* the questions."

Concern drifted into the corners of her eyes, and Liam knew that he wasn't going to press her about what she'd almost said earlier regarding the way she grew up. This was date one, and they'd gone from her laying him out onto the mat for touching her, all the way to stolen kisses that had his cock hardening just in remembrance of her lips on his.

He could afford to be patient, to keep things light, to gain her trust.

To help her have some fun.

Because even though they'd just met, he knew this woman was beyond deserving of it, and he also had the distinct thought that she'd had far too little of it in her life.

"Want a sample question?" he asked before she could panic too much. Before he lost her beneath those shields of steel again.

She made a face.

"That's not a no," he said, reaching across and running his finger down her nose. "Okay, so here goes. This is a biggie. A hugely important, make or break, it's all over if you answer incorrectly—"

"Um—"

"—question," he continued, ignoring the interruption. "Chunky or smooth peanut butter?"

Those lickable lips had parted, no doubt readying another protest, but his question had them freezing in place, the pink tip of her tongue darting out to moisten the bottom one. Then his words processed, and she shook her head. "You enjoy tormenting me, don't you?"

"Hey," he protested. "This is life or death stuff."

A roll of her eyes. "Smooth peanut butter. Obviously."

He lifted his hand, palm out. "Damn right. Okay, your turn."

"Hmm." She tapped a finger to her chin. "Tell me the truth. Do you break your diet and eat sugar on non-Cheat Days?"

"Honestly?" he asked.

"That's a requirement."

"No, I don't," he said. "It was hard as hell those first few weeks, and I'll admit I do go a bit crazy with it when I'm allowed. But I'm not going to fuck up my career because I want a cookie."

She shifted in the booth and her leg brushed his, sending sparks flying. "That's good."

"Why did you ask?"

A shrug. "You don't seem like much of a rule follower is all."

"My family would be surprised to hear that," he told her. "I'm the youngest, but I was left to my own devices for a lot of my childhood. I always do better in environments with clear expectations and rules."

"Just not signs?"

He reached across the table, snagged her hand. "Most of that was because I really love the way you look when you're outraged."

She gasped and snatched her fingers free.

Liam captured them, lifted her hand to his mouth and pressed a fleeting kiss to her knuckles. "See?" he said. "Just like that."

"You're impossible."

"As long as you like impossible and are willing to put up with it."

"Liam," she murmured.

"No pressure," he said, releasing her hand when she tugged back.

"It's not—" She shook her head. "I'm not normal. I'm not a typical woman who's going to melt and bat her eyelashes and tell you what you want to hear."

"Good thing I don't like normal."

Mia sighed. "I don't think—"

"*Don't* think," he said. "Just take some time *not* thinking and let's just have fun and ride slides and eat pancakes—or, well, egg-white omelets." He reached out and squeezed her hand. "This doesn't have to be heavy or intense. We can just do . . . *this*."

Quiet.

A long moment of quiet as intense brown eyes studied him. He told himself to keep being patient, to let her come to her own decision, but when she started to shake her head again, when he knew, instinctively, she was going to cut this down before it even started, and he couldn't keep quiet.

Liam knew he didn't want to let this woman go.

She was a puzzle. She was smart. She was beautiful.

He'd be a fucking moron to let that just walk away from him.

"It's okay to have fun," he said.

Solemn chocolate eyes. "You wouldn't say that if you really knew me."

"I—"

The waiter returned then, setting their plates in front of them, asking if they needed anything else, but Liam barely heard him. Because he might not have pushed learning about her upbringing, but he needed to understand what she meant—

"I'm not going to talk about it," she said.

Cool words. Challenge in that gaze now.

And he knew if he pushed, she would get right up and walk out of the restaurant. Leave her omelet, leave him, and not look back.

That pissed him off, was beyond infuriating.

Except . . . he hadn't earned the right to demand anything from this woman. Not one fucking thing. Trust took time to build, and they weren't even at one full day yet. So, he stifled the urge to push, to find out what had made the shadows fill her eyes, understand the pain that deepened the lines around her mouth.

Instead, he held tight to his patience.

"Okay," he said, not-so-smoothly changing the subject. "Critical question number two is: What do I have to do to get you to come on that slide with me again?"

Her shoulders had crept up with each word, but by the time he finished the question, they'd relaxed, her lips curving, her eyes rolling. "That's not going to happen."

"Fine." He dumped the container of syrup on his pancakes, mixing it with the whipped cream that was smothered on top. Then he picked up his fork and scooped a forkful into his mouth. Sweet baby Jesus, sweet and sour, acidic and creamy, his taste buds did a happy dance because that was absolutely fucking delicious. "Then what do I need to do to get you to try a bit of this ambrosia?"

Mia made a face. "It looks like it'll give me diabetes."

"I'll try a bite of yours."

"I don't think that'll be a trial for you, considering your diet."

He gave her innocent eyes. "But it's my Cheat Day."

"I don't like sugar, Liam." She took a dainty bite of her

omelet. "Exposing me to more of it isn't going to make me like it more."

"Are you sure?" he asked. "I was thinking it was like iocaine powder." He took another huge bite, chewed, and swallowed. "You just need to slowly build it up in your system until you start liking it."

"Did you just try to slide a *Princess Bride* reference into our conversation?"

"Maybe." He lifted a brow. "All right, sugar aside, please tell me that you're in the camp that likes *The Princess Bride?*"

She scoffed. "There are people who *don't* like it?"

"Heathens," he confirmed.

"I can't believe it." She put down her fork and tucked a strand of hair that had escaped her ponytail behind her ear. "How can anyone not like it? That movie is an absolute classic. 'No more rhyming and I mean it.'"

"'Anybody want a peanut?'" he dutifully finished.

"Yes!" she exclaimed. "Exactly. So many good things. 'Is this a kissing book?', 'As you wish!', 'Twue Wuv.' There's so much pop culture in a tiny, two-hour package."

Movies. She liked movies. She liked romcoms. Well, or at least the best romcom ever.

Liam smothered a grin, filing away the insight. "Have you read the book?"

"Uh, yes," she said, the 'duh' unspoken but still audible to his ears.

"What'd you think?"

"The book is always better," she said, stating it like the fact it was. "But that movie damn near approached perfection."

"Speaking of book-movie adaptations, what did you think of. . ." He named a big-name blockbuster that had recently come out. The book had been a worldwide success, and the movie was highly anticipated.

"I haven't seen it yet." She sighed. "I want to, but I didn't get to the theater last weekend."

He resisted the urge to crow in triumph. She might not like sugar. She might not break or bend the rules, but Mia had at least one vice—and it was movies. "I haven't seen it either," he said. "I guess that means you have to come with me. I don't play on Friday."

Her eyes widened, but she didn't shrink into herself or back down. In fact, her expression shifted to considering. "I don't have classes on Friday nights."

He knew that.

He'd memorized the schedule taped to the door of her studio.

"So you'll come with me?" he asked. "I hate going to the movies by myself."

Narrowed eyes on his. "You won't talk during the film?"

"Absolutely not," he said, adding and meaning it with every fiber of his being. "Number one pet peeve is people who talk during movies."

That earned him a smile. "If you're lying—"

"I'm not, J.B." He grinned at her. "Come with me? Please? I'll even spring for popcorn."

"I don't eat popcorn."

Why didn't that surprise him?

Liam sighed.

She giggled. "But I'll still let you buy a bucket." A beat. "So long as it's a Cheat Day."

Damn. He hadn't thought of that.

And Mia knew that, because she giggled again, a light sound that made him feel about ten feet tall. "Friday it is, Sweet Cheeks," she said. "And maybe I'll get some popcorn for myself just to torture you with."

He laughed.

She laughed.

Then they finished their meals, chatting about favorite movies, discovering that more often than not, they had the same likes and dislikes. She was pretty and fun when she relaxed, with a self-deprecating edge that tempered her barbed wit. He *liked* her, liked her more with each minute he spent with her.

So much so, that by the time Liam paid and walked Mia back to her studio, he was half in love with her already.

So much so, that when he waved goodbye through the glass after somehow finagling her into giving him her number, he knew he'd be counting down the minutes until he could see her again.

So much so, that he sent her a text the moment he sat down in his car.

Too much?

Probably.

But just as he could tell that Mia needed to have a little fun, he also knew that she needed care.

And he was going to give it to her.

—————

He shoved his feet into his skates, taking a few minutes to make sure the laces were perfectly tightened.

Too much would create something called skate bite, and it was brutal. It made the tops of the feet ache and burn, long after the skates were loosened to the proper tightness. Liam spent too much time with these blades strapped to his body to not have them just perfect.

So, not too tight.

And not too loose—because they wouldn't give him enough support to sprint and change direction.

It was the Goldilocks syndrome of skate tying.

But thankfully, he'd been on the ice since he was just over a year old. First, with his dad holding him up as he just walked across the ice in the tiniest pair of skates imaginable. Flying by the time he was three. Fearless. Fast. The product of a hockey dynasty.

Ha.

Perhaps culmination was the proper term.

Either way—the ruin or realization—it meant that Liam

had twenty-four years of skate tying experience—minus a few years, he supposed, before he'd learned how to do tie them himself.

Some might even say he was an expert.

He grinned, thinking that Mia would have had a pert comeback to that statement, just on principle.

"It's nice to see you smiling."

Blinking, he glanced up, saw Brit was looking at him. "Sorry, what?" he asked.

She bent, tying her own skates. "You've seemed a bit—" A shake of her head, words cut off. "Never mind me. I'm being nosy. The guys have corrupted me."

Max, one of their defensemen, who'd been around the league, and the Gold, for years now, snorted and shook his head. "The *guys* have corrupted you?" he asked. "The *guys?* You're the nosiest of them all."

Blane was in the next stall down on Liam's other side. "That's a fine distinction in this room."

Brit straightened, pointed a finger at Blane. "Hey! I grew up with you, but you're older. So, if I'm nosy, then I learned those skills from you."

"Whatever you say," Blane muttered, standing and shrugging into his jersey.

"Words a woman dreams to hear," Brit quipped.

A flash of a smile from Blane. "I know. Mandy"—his wife and one of the Gold's physical therapists—"tells me that frequently."

"The question is," Liam said dryly, "do you listen?"

Quiet descended.

A long, uncomfortable silence that had Blane, Max, and Brit staring at him like he had two heads—or maybe that he'd overstepped, he realized with a sinking sensation. He was the newcomer here, hadn't yet earned the right to tease or poke fun. Picked up just a few weeks ago, he definitely hadn't been contributing to the scoresheet.

A black hole. A weak spot.

The words, in a familiar hard voice, pounded through his brain.

Liam opened his mouth, apology on the tip of his tongue.

"Holy. Shit," Brit breathed. "You made a joke. I don't believe it."

Max started laughing. "Come on, he's not that bad, just a little quiet."

"I didn't say he was bad," Brit said. "I just said he made a joke, and it's awesome."

"I don't believe you used the word *awesome*," Max said.

"Okay, so maybe I didn't use that exact word—"

"You didn't," Coop, their star forward, chimed in from a few spots down. "End of story."

Brit scowled. "You—"

Max grinned. "Because I think you *actually* said—"

"Ah!" Brit jumped to her feet, one skate tied, the other with the laces dangling, and reached out, pretending like she was going to strangle him.

Liam fussed with his laces, even though they were already perfect.

The nudge on his right arm had him glancing up again, seeing that Blane had sat back down and was looking at him with a gaze that said he saw more than Liam had intended to show.

Fuck, he was a mess.

"It might have been a mediocre joke," Blane said lightly, flashing a smile that had gotten him more than a few endorsement deals over the last years, "but I *am* glad you made it." His voice dropped. "Have you settled in okay? You've seemed—"

Liam held his breath, waiting for the derision to sink into Blane's tone. He'd heard enough of it over the years to know that it always did, and that even though someone might seem nice off the ice, in all of the media the various teams did, mean still crept through in the off the record moments.

"—sad," Blane finished, which was pretty much the last adjective Liam had expected to hear. "Is everything okay home-wise? I know making a transition to a new team, a new state can be tough."

Words.

They were hard sometimes.

He stared at Blane, trying to reconcile what the other man was saying with his expectations of what he'd thought he was about to hear. The Gold had a reputation for being like a family, for being a group of teammates who looked after one another. Except . . . Liam hadn't really believed it. He'd played on teams who were supposed to be like family, and fuck, if *they* had been family, it had made his own semi-dysfunctional one look like the Brady Bunch.

He'd assumed the Gold was like that.

Creative marketing on the surface.

Plenty of fucked up beneath.

"Sorry," Blane said, leaning back. "I'm getting to be as bad as *that* crew"—he nodded at Max and Brit, who were still bickering over something, though it sounded now like the argument had shifted from Liam to a playlist of some sort. Coop was mostly watching them fight, adding the odd comment here or there.

"It's horrible," Max moaned. "The whole playlist."

"You know the rules," Brit said. "The fastest gets to pick."

"All well and good when you're always the fastest," Coop said, tone dry, though there was amusement in his expression.

"Them's the rules," she said.

"And who *made* the rules?" Max asked.

"Anyway," she said, waving a hand and ignoring him. "My point is that the song makes me run faster." A beat, lips twitching. "Thus, it *has* to stay in."

"You don't *need* to run faster," Max muttered. "You're already too damned fast as it is."

Blane sighed and shook his head. "Sometimes I feel like I'm back in peewees," he grumbled, but his lips were twitching. "Still, I hope you'll forgive my next bit of nosy-as-fuck, but joke away, man. No one is too big or important for it here. Don't worry about hurting feelings. Just be you."

"I—" Liam stopped, not quite knowing what to say. He wasn't a rookie. He'd been around the league a while, and though —obviously—he'd never quite found his place . . . Blane seemed to know that.

Cool.

He was the pathetic guy everyone felt sorry for—

Enough.

The word was harsh enough through his mind that he jerked slightly.

Fuck, was he just going to keep doing this? He'd spent the previous morning with a woman who was rigid and unflappable at first glance but had so many deeper emotions beneath the surface—fearful but soft, scared but determined, fragile but not breakable. Yet, she'd let him push her outside her comfort zone, had taken steps to do it herself.

So, was Liam really just going to play it safe and do the same old shit?

Stay in the same cycle? Piss away what might be his last months as a professional hockey player?

Fuck. Just . . . *enough.*

He missed loving the game from the moment he stepped on the ice. He missed joking with his teammates. He missed the rush that came from making a good play or seeing a linemate score. He missed the relief that overpowered the demands of his lungs, his heart, his mind when he hauled ass back to stop his goalie from facing a two-on-O. He missed . . . the sport.

And if he was only going to have a few months left then, for the first time in years, he wanted to make those months count. He was less scared of fucking up and more scared of never getting back what he'd lost. Because one thing was clear, this half-life, this playing on the fringes and just barely hanging on, wasn't enough anymore.

"Anyway, I know the room is a little different with Mike and Stefan retired now. We've tried to keep the vibe the same." A shrug. "We all play better when we're relaxed and messing around

—off the ice, that is. Loosens that hold on our sticks enough to focus on the system, on being creative and improvising rather than being so scared to make a mistake that we're robots more than artists."

"Robots more than *artists?*" Brit said, on the other side of Liam, suddenly tuning in to their conversation. Her voice was incredulous. "Blane"—she clamped a hand to her chest—"oh my. You're a poet."

Max and Coop snickered.

Blane rolled his eyes, but he was smiling . . . especially when he locked gazes with Liam for a heartbeat before reaching up and balling a sock, launching it at Brit's head.

Since she was prattling on about poetry while sharing smirking sentiments with Max, she didn't see it coming.

"Hey!" she exclaimed when it nailed her in the temple.

Liam snorted, biting back a grin.

At least until Blane pointed at him and said, "He did it."

"I—"

But before he could muster more than that syllable, Brit picked up the sock and threw it back at Blane, who caught it easily. "Don't worry, Li," she said. "I wasn't joking about growing up together. I know how that one's"—narrowed eyes at Blane—"dirty ass socks smell. Fuckers could rouse the dead."

Blane launched the sock back, but Brit saw it coming this time, and thus caught it easily. "Ha!" she said. "All that glove hand practice does me good."

She wound up again, and Liam found himself interjecting again. "Maybe we should take that glove hand onto the ice," he said. "Practice starts in five." He nodded at the clock that hung over the door.

Brit made a face. "Fine," she said, tossing the sock back to Blane. "Be reasonable, why don't you?"

Blane snorted, shoving the sock ball back into his shoe. "That's in short supply with this team."

"Hey!" Max said.

"Pot meet kettle," Coop added, getting up and heading to the door.

Liam saw why a second later, when Calle, one of the team's assistant coaches and Coop's wife, poked her head in through the doorway and called. "Let's hit it, boys!"

"Shit," Brit muttered, dropping to her knees and buckling her leg pads with the same rapid efficiency that Liam had used on his skates. Years and years of muscle memory that ensured they'd be fastened exactly right. After, she stood and started strapping on her chest protector as he was working on his elbow pads.

They slipped their jerseys over their heads at almost the same moment, Brit grinning as she fixed her long blonde ponytail. "You're kind of fast, Williamson."

"Um, thanks?" he said. "You, too?"

A beatific smile. "Yeah. And you know what that means?"

"Oh no," Max mumbled, but Brit was still talking, and Liam was focused on her words.

"It means, you're officially invited to run with us."

"Oh no," Max moaned. "Abort. *Abort!*"

Brit punched him. "Stop," she said. "Coop promised me earlier that he was coming, too. Plus, it's fun!"

"It's something," Blane muttered, standing and heading out the door. Still, he paused and looked back. "Straight after practice?"

Brit nodded. "Yup. Gear off. Stairs on."

Max groaned. "Oh God."

"I'll be there," Blane said before he disappeared into the hall.

"Max?" she asked.

"Heaven help me for peer pressure, but yes."

She fist-pumped, turned her bright blue eyes on him. "Liam?"

He shoved his hands into his gloves, wondered for a moment what he was getting himself into and if it was possible that he'd screw up whatever Brit wanted from him. But . . . *no.* He was sticking with it. Fuck it. This was nice. The teasing. The poking fun. The insult-trading.

Maybe that gave an insight to how fucked up he was inside, that he liked the insults and wanted more. But again . . . fuck it.

If these were his last months, then he was going to do what he wanted.

He was curious. They'd invited him. He was going to stop worrying and start putting some words to action. "Okay," he said, nodding, excited rather than dreading . . . and if he'd known the fate he'd just ensured himself, then Liam definitely would have been dreading.

"Yes!" Another fist-pump. "Lose the gear, trade skates for sneakers, and meet at the PT Suite after practice." She walked to the door.

Max clapped him on the shoulder as he made his way out. "Man." A shake of his head. "You just signed your death warrant."

"What?" Liam asked.

"Of course, it'll be worth it in the end," Max said, "but still. Death. Warrant."

"What—"

Before he could finish the question, Max disappeared.

He chalked it up to more joking, but yeah, if Liam had known what was awaiting him on those stairs, he definitely would have taken Max's words much more seriously. As it was, he spent practice loose and relaxed and looking forward to something hockey-teammate-related for the first time in a long while.

And he found that looking forward to something took his mind off his game.

That morning, he played like he once had.

Creative. Strong. Self-assured.

He played like *himself*. Before his love of the game had been shrunk down to nothing, before his confidence had been eaten away by coaching, by teammates, by his own brain, before family responsibility had trumped enjoyment.

But . . . if only he'd know what was coming his way after practice.

———

A couple of hours later, he collapsed to the floor alongside Max, Coop, and Blane, chest heaving, legs shaking. "I don't . . . know what . . . was more . . . torturous," he said, gasping in air, "Brit's pace . . . or the music."

"The music, dude," Max said, lying back, his arms extending over his head, trying to suck in more air.

"Why are you guys always so tired?" Brit asked, barely out of breath even though she'd led them on an intense sprint through the bleachers that surrounded the practice rink. Up, down, over. Up, down, over. Again and again between each set.

And then around a second time because apparently these bleachers were smaller than the other place they usually ran, the team's home arena, the Gold Mine, and they'd needed to be "balanced."

"You should be getting in better shape," she said, taking a dainty sip of water.

Liam was the first to recover, and he pushed to his feet, stretching out his trembling legs.

"We *are* in better shape," Blane said with a groan then mirrored Max by sprawling out on the ground, arms overhead.

"The problem is that you are, too," Coop added.

Liam could see that. Brit had moved like liquid lightning over the stairs. The pace had been brutal, she'd sprinted past them and hadn't let up the entire time they'd run. Yet, here she was calmly stretching out her quads, her forehead lightly glistening with sweat, her cheeks flushed pink from exertion but having already caught her breath. She looked like a freaking angel.

Meanwhile, he felt like he'd been pulled backward through a hedge.

She'd thoroughly kicked his ass, and done it effortlessly.

He thought of another woman who'd *already* kicked his ass effortlessly. Only this one had long black hair and careful brown eyes. A mouth that had tasted like heaven and temptation all at once—

"Mia would like you," he said, lost in his brain, not realizing he'd spoken the words out loud until Brit's head whipped toward him, eyes calculating.

"Who's Mia?"

Alarm bells blared through Liam's brain.

He turned to see Max, Coop, and Blane sit up, equally calculating.

Uh-oh.

———

It was late on the East Coast. Too late for his dad to be calling, but his father was a force of nature. He didn't respect boundaries or silly things like time zones.

Liam let the call go to voicemail, knew at some point he'd need to talk to his family, but he couldn't deny that the distance between New York and California had actually turned out to be a good thing. It had given him space, allowed him a chance to regroup.

His phone began buzzing again almost immediately, but Liam still didn't answer the call.

The reason why came precisely two seconds after the second call.

Buzz-buzz.

Good last game. Keep your head up and your elbows out, it'll give you more space on the entry.

The advice was fine. It was good. It would probably help.

The trouble was that the advice didn't stop there.

The messages kept buzzing through. Two. Four. Seven texts in all.

Six too many, especially considering the first text didn't end after *Good last game.*

Liam sighed, knew he'd need to figure out to handle his dad—perhaps, he'd get his mom to run interference? Sometimes that garnered him a few weeks' break. But either way, he needed a break from thinking about the Williamsons and their legacy of hockey, of all the ways he needed to improve, about everything he was doing wrong.

He needed to forget hockey for the moment.

Especially since there was a certain black-eyed beauty he was desperate to talk to.

Eight

Mia

She was just reaching for the light switch, readying to flick it off and head up to her apartment to cook dinner for herself, when her cell phone rang.

Her heart skipped a beat.

Silly, it was probably just a telemarketer, but she couldn't stop herself from hoping that it would be Liam.

He'd texted her a couple of times yesterday, but he'd had practice today, and other than a quick good morning, she hadn't heard from him. She *shouldn't* have heard from him, not when they hardly knew each—

"Isn't that argument getting old?" she muttered to herself, tugging out her phone.

It was.

Because . . . as much as it didn't make sense, Mia felt connected to Liam in a way she'd never felt tied to another person.

So, steeling herself for the disappointment that was sure to come—because no one actually called her aside from telemarketers—she glanced at the screen.

And then felt that little tendril of hope plant itself firmly in her heart.

Liam's name was on the screen.

She swiped a finger across it to answer the call, brought it up to her ear. "Hello?"

"Hi, J.B."

Heat arrowing between her thighs, but she was made of sterner stuff. "When are you going to tell me what that means?"

"How are you?" he asked, neatly avoiding the question. There was noise in the background, the sounds of a restaurant with multiple voices overlapping, the tinkle of silverware against plates.

"I'm good," she said. "Classes are done."

"I know."

She found herself leaning against the wall, loving the way his slightly rasping voice trailed over her skin. "You know?"

"Your last class finished at eight-thirty," he said.

Yes, it had.

"Then you had to clean up," he went on.

Yes, she had.

"Sorry, I didn't finish here in time to come see you like I'd planned."

Mia froze. There was a lot to decipher in that statement. "What?"

"I'm at a charity thing. Brit roped me in because Blane had to flake. His daughter spiked a fever—" He broke off on a chuckle. "Not a hundred percent sure what that means," he admitted, "but I know enough to understand that fevers aren't good."

"Yes," she agreed.

"Anyway." He sighed. "I'm here. You're there."

"Terrible," she said, going for a joke.

A soft, husky laugh. "It is," he said. "I was going to tempt you into another kiss."

Her breath caught, a curl of desire sliding through her stomach. She knew she would have let him kiss her. There was no tempting necessary. Still, circling back to strong, to steel. "You could try."

A pause then, voice deeper now, with a trace of heat, "What would tempt you?"

Every *single* thing about this man.

She bit her tongue, stifling admitting that, and instead said, "Cleaning."

Another pause, longer this time. "Cleaning?"

"Yup," Mia said. "Cleaning shows responsibility. Initiative. Follow-through. Those are all tempting characteristics."

"Hmm." A heated rumble. "And did you . . . clean tonight?"

She stopped, considered her answer. He'd somehow made that sound dirty, but her mind wasn't working fast enough for her to come up with a witty response. Instead what came out was, "You know I did. The pads were dirty."

"Yes. They were dirty." His voice dropped further, sliding right down her spine and into her panties. "And if I'd been there, would you have let me help?"

How did the man make a conversation about cleaning sound sexy?

Well, come on, Mia, her mind snapped, pulling her back into herself. *You practically gave him that one with the whole 'dirty' thing.*

True.

She caught a glimpse of herself in the mirror and made a face. "Well, since I'm not stupid enough to refuse help for the dreaded task of mat cleaning, yes, I would have allowed you to assist." Ice had drifted into her words, but he didn't seem to mind. In fact, she could almost feel him smiling through the speaker.

"Hmm," he said again, still hot, still sending prickles of heat through her, "and did I do a good job of *assisting* you the other night?"

She sniffed. "It was adequate."

He laughed outright. "I missed talking to you today, J.B."

"I don't think I like that nickname."

"I think *I* like you."

"Ugh."

More smiles through the airwaves. She didn't know how she knew that, just felt it in her gut. "Why *ugh?*"

"You're being charming."

"Not sure that's a bad thing," he said, "especially when the more important question is . . . is the charming working?"

She yawned, the lack of sleep from two nights before still catching up to her, and flicked off the light, heading into her office, then upstairs to her apartment. "Some would say I'm uncharmable."

"Guess I'd better up my game."

"I guess you'd better." Mia locked the door at the top of the stairs then crossed through the short hall that led to the apartment's back entrance. "Tell me about this fundraiser." She let herself in, threw the dead bolt behind her, then headed to her bedroom, toeing off her shoes before shoving down her sweats.

"Are you—?" For the first time he sounded shocked. His voice dropped to a hiss. "Are you undressing?"

She went ramrod still. "What?"

"I heard rustling."

"I—" Her pants were around her ankles, but she didn't know what to do. She'd been on autopilot, going through her normal routine of exchanging her clothes for her pajamas. "Yes," she said. Fuck it, she wasn't going to hide what she was doing. Not from this man, not anymore.

"How much begging do I need to do to get you to switch to FaceTime?"

"Too much."

"Damn. If I can't get a visual, then at least tell me where you're changing. Your office, so I can get sexy office porn vibes? Or in front of those mirrors? They're very 1990s gym class sexy."

Her mouth fell open, and she stood with her sweats draped over her feet, totally thrown for a loop. "Are you serious right now?"

"No." He laughed. "Though, let it be stated that I'm not opposed to seeing you naked."

She snorted and shook her head then stepped out of her pants. "You're incorrigible."

"That's my middle name," he quipped.

"I'm in my apartment."

"Oh," he said. "I thought you were still in the studio."

"Don't you have to get back to that fundraiser?"

"No," he told her. "I did my part. I'm just waiting for Brit to finish her conversation so we can go." The noise behind his voice went a little quieter. "Now tell me, you live close by the studio? Since you're already getting naked?"

A huff. "I'm not naked!"

"Let a man have his fantasies."

She rolled her eyes. "I'm standing by my incorrigible statement." A sigh when he didn't reply other than a soft chuckle. "Yes, you could say I live close," she told him. "I live above the studio."

"Oh."

Mia waited for him to say more. "Just *oh?*"

"You said I'm incorrigible." She waited, and the troublesome man stayed right on course with his next reply. "So, I'm not going to tell you all the fantasies that just went through my mind."

Except, even *that* was enough to make her want. "Liam."

She heard the voices rise in the background. "Fuck, Brit's coming," he muttered. "And I didn't even get to the point of me calling."

"Why did you call?"

"I wanted to make sure you didn't chicken out on Friday."

She huffed in outrage. "I don't chicken out."

"The slide?" was his only response.

She growled, yanked open her pajama drawer and stepped into the plain blue cotton bottoms. "I don't chicken out on things that are *legal*."

A beat then, "Okay, that's fair."

"Exactly."

"I also wanted—" The rest of his sentence was lost as the voices grew in volume again.

"Also wanted what?" she asked, raising his voice. "Liam?"

"Sorry," he said, "I had to hide in the closet."

"Hiding in the closet? Why?"

He cursed softly. "Because my teammates are nosy as fuck and want to know if I'm talking to *the* Mia."

The Mia?

Her throat went tight. What the hell did that mean?

"Come to the game tomorrow."

She was still reeling from *the* Mia. "I—"

"The game doesn't start until seven-thirty. Your classes end at six-thirty. I can send a car, get you a ticket in the lower bowl—"

"Liam—"

"Please, say you'll come."

"Why?"

"Why?" he asked.

"Yes," she said. "*Why?*"

Quiet stretched between them.

"Promise you won't panic if I tell you?"

"No," she said, her heart threatening to pound its way out of her chest. What was he going to tell her? That he loved her and wanted her forever? It was way too soon for such sentiments, and also that was . . . terrifying—although probably not as terrifying as it reasonably should have been. More likely, he was going to tell her he needed to imagine her hard-ass head on the puck in order to hit it really hard. Centered by the last thought, she said, "I absolutely will not promise to not panic."

He laughed, and it coated her skin like honey. "Fuck," he said, "but I like you, Mia."

"Why, Liam?" she pressed.

A sigh then his voice dropped. "Because I want to look in the crowd and know someone is there for me. *Just* for me."

Her breath caught because . . . well, it wasn't what she

expected. But also, it was so much *more* than she'd anticipated hearing. "I like you, too," she whispered.

"I'm glad, J.B." A beat. "So, will you come?"

"I don't need a car," she said.

"Okay."

"And I'll buy my own ticket."

"The game's sold out."

"Fine," she said. "I'll reimburse you for the cost."

"No."

"*Liam,*" she warned.

A sigh. "Fine," he said, giving in easier than she would have expected. He didn't seem like the kind of man who'd let a woman pay for something he wanted. But then again, she hardly knew him, maybe she'd misread that particular facet of his personality.

"Okay, I'll come."

"Really?" he asked, and it was hard to ignore the way her heart swelled with something soft, something tender in the same spot that the tendril of hope had made itself at home earlier.

"Really," she said.

"Thanks, sweetheart."

She didn't know if she liked that endearment or J.B. better. Both make her breathing hitch, filled her with warmth. Both made that spot in her heart expand. "You're welcome," Mia said, matter of fact now, pushing the feelings aside to ponder later. "Now, how much is the ticket?"

"Free."

Irritation coursed through her. "Liam."

"No, seriously," he said. "It's comped."

She sighed. "*That's* why you were all fine with me paying for it?"

"Maybe."

Mia couldn't help it. She laughed. "Text me the ticket, you incorrigible man." Then, just to show him—and perhaps, also to show herself—she added, "I have to go get naked now."

She hung up to the sound of his groan.

———

The next day, Mia scanned her cell's screen at the entrance to the Gold Mine then made her way through the crowd, up an escalator and onto the concourse. She didn't stop to buy anything except a bottle of water, having snagged a quick and healthy meal that didn't cost fifty bucks and was better than the mediocre food she could buy at the arena anyway.

Not *much* better, but her steamed broccoli, carrots, and shredded chicken was healthy and filling . . . and way less than an —her eyes caught the food pricing as she snagged her six-dollar bottle of water—eighteen-dollar personal pizza that was approximately the size of a postage stamp.

Next time, if there was a next time, she'd have to see if there was a water fountain.

Not only was the disposable plastic bad, but *six* dollars for a bottle of water.

Good God. The markup.

Still, the eating at home had been part control (that was her norm, her routine), and part . . . penance.

Because she'd spent the last few days with too much fluff.

If her dad were alive, he would hate it. He'd frown in disapproval. He'd glare and be furious. But even if he had still been alive, Mia thought she would still be at this game.

There was something about Liam. They—and fuck this made her sound totally insane, she knew—but they seemed to unlock something in each other.

Her sharp made him grin.

His pushiness made her bend.

And . . . he was fun.

So, maybe this would end in heartbreak—and if she let the realistic part of her mind take over, she thought it was likely she *would* end up with a broken heart. But also, maybe she'd find a way to stop being stuck in this stasis and move forward.

Maybe she'd find a way to forgive herself.

Her eyes caught on a huge banner congratulating the Gold on having captured the Cup the season before, and she thought her dad would have loved to be here at this game.

One, because the ticket was free.

Two, because he'd loved hockey and had been thrilled to see San Francisco get a team.

Too bad he'd died before he'd made it to a game.

Too bad he'd died still resenting her.

"Fuck," she muttered under her breath, so used to working with kids that she'd made the word inaudible to all but herself. She'd done enough in her twenty-six years, she did not have to add being the person who'd taught someone's kid the f-word to her resumé.

Thankfully, thinking about kids and the f-word was enough to snap her out of her brain, allowed her to tuck the memories back down.

There was nothing she could do to go back and fix things.

She had to move forward, to live a life her father would be proud of now.

Mia mentally nodded then went to find a bathroom and make her way to her seat. As she walked down the aisle, searching the ticket on her cell's screen for the seat and row number—the first time she'd bothered to look at anything other than the section— she realized that Liam had gotten her a seat right on the glass.

"Jesus Fucking Christ," she muttered, breaking two of her rules in approximately one-point-two-seconds. First, there was a child in front of her, who heard the f-bomb and promptly repeated it. Second, her father had been proud of thriftiness, of the essentials, of nothing superfluous. A front-row seat was the opposite of that in every sense.

Except . . . her dad had loved hockey.

So, maybe this would be okay? Especially since it hadn't cost anything.

She bit back another curse and clenched her free hand into a tight fist, trying to calm herself, to find the control she drilled into her kids. Grabbing on to it by the narrowest of margins, she apologized to the child's mother, took a deep breath, and made her way down to the front row.

The ice had been empty as she made her way down, but almost the moment her ass hit the seat, both teams came out for their warm-ups.

Mia watched the steady stream of players as they skated by the glass, amazed that most of them seemed so big, even though the ice was well below the level of the floor where her seat was positioned. She supposed it was the extra few inches the skates added. Well, that along with the padding. Liam was taller than her, more muscular, but most of the guys out there were still bigger.

She couldn't be sure if Liam's size was an advantage or disadvantage.

Maybe he'd have more maneuverability than the bigger guys. She did remember him being fast. But he might not be able to out-body one of the giants on the boards or off the puck.

Though . . . she considered that carefully. She often sparred against men who were bigger, who were stronger.

It took strategy rather than strength to win in those cases.

And Liam had made the big leagues. Despite his indication that his contract wouldn't be renewed, the way he'd winced when she'd said she'd seen the game, he *had* to be talented.

Which also brought the question as to why she was there.

Had something changed? Had he gotten an offer after all?

Or had what he'd told her the night before—him wanting a person in the stands just for him—been the whole truth?

She wasn't sure.

Anyway, she didn't have time to ponder further, because the steady stream of black-jersey-wearing had slowed to a trickle, or at least slowed enough that she could start picking out names and faces. Brayden's, her student helper's, dad was in one corner, a huge grin on his face. Max looked to be joking with another player, whose name she struggled to remember.

"Hart," she whispered to herself. "Blane Hart."

Brit Plantain was in the net, her long blonde ponytail bisecting her last name and the numbers on the back of her jersey.

Mia's eyes flicked around the ice, caught sight of Coop Armstrong, Blue Anderson, and Kevin Hayes. All big names who'd hoisted the Cup the last time the team had won it.

But where was Liam?

Her eyes searched the players stretching on the opposite side of the ice, the ones circling the next and shooting pucks at Brit in net. None were Liam.

Then she heard the *tap-tap*.

Her eyes flew from the far boards up to the man standing just to the side of her view. When their gazes connected, Liam shifted a little bit, just enough to block his teammates out, just enough that for a few seconds it felt as though the rest of the world had disappeared and it was just the two of them.

Then Coop skated over and nudged Liam out of the way.

He glanced at Mia and waved, flashing a smile that was movie star worthy. She found herself waving back, instinctively catching the puck that he tossed over.

Without a second thought, she handed it to a little boy who'd come down to watch the players warm-up and who was waving frantically at Liam, at Coop, at any Gold player that skated by. The black-haired kiddo was all of about four and ridiculously cute, and the smile he gave her when she handed him the puck stole her heart.

Then he was running off, back up the stairs, an excited, "Mom! Look!" reaching her ears.

When Mia glanced back, Coop was gone, but Liam was still there.

She shrugged and smiled. He grinned, mouthed, "Hi, J.B."

She scowled.

He waved, inclined his head over his shoulder, and she nodded, mouthed back, "Good luck."

Entranced, she watched him skate, saw how effortless he looked, how smooth and graceful. He was definitely smaller than the rest of the guys, but he wasn't the only one. Coop had a few inches on him but was lean as well. Blane, meanwhile, was built like a tank, along with Kevin.

They looked like they could eat Liam for breakfast.

And she'd barely spared a glance for their opponent, the Kings.

Then it was too late to scope out the competition. The buzzer rang, the teams exited the ice, and the lights dimmed as a pair of Zambonis came out to resurface the ice.

There was an entire crew working once the teams disappeared —the drivers of the machines that smoothed out the divots and laid fresh water to freeze on top of the existing ice, people on the benches stocking water bottles, smelling salts, and extra equipment. A pair of men in a box that held announcing equipment. Several people walking the ice, visually inspecting it, and shooting out small streams of water as they moved.

Lots of moving parts. So many balls being juggled. A ton of tasks happening at once.

And everyone doing their job.

She loved it.

"Excuse me?"

Mia tore her eyes from the ice and turned to face the young girl holding a black tray and wearing a Gold T-shirt. "Hi," she said.

"These are for you." The girl extended the tray.

"Oh," Mia said. "I didn't order anything—"

"There's a note," the girl said, thrusting the tray at her. "Sorry, I have more deliveries to make."

"I—"

But the girl was gone.

"Okay," she murmured, staring down at the plastic tray. It held a tub of popcorn, a beer, a pretzel, and a sundae with about a gallon of hot fudge on it. But tucked under the popcorn was indeed an envelope.

With her name written clearly on the outside of it.

Fumbling, she set the tray beneath her feet and freed the note, knowing in her heart who it was from, and feeling the tendril of hope and connection in her heart growing deeper, stronger.

With trembling fingers, she tore open the flap and read. The note was short, sweet, and made her lips curve into the biggest smile.

Just because it's not my cheat day, doesn't mean it can't be yours.
-L
P.S. Come on. You know you like popcorn. Indulge in that buttery goodness.
P.P.S. You're allowed a little fluff every once in a while.
P.P.S.S. Come to the elevator outside of Section 101 after the game. Please?

This was more than a *little* fluff. It was . . . well, a trayful.

And she hadn't been lying about the popcorn thing at the movies. She didn't eat it. Too salty. Too fatty. Too buttery and cholesterol-inducing. Both of her parents had agreed on that.

But . . . the "buttery goodness" did smell good.

Maybe it was the cold, icy air. Maybe it was that Liam had bought it for her. Either way, she found herself reaching extending a hand and picking up one of the fluffy kernels between thumb and forefinger, found herself popping it into her mouth and—

An explosion of flavors. Yes, it was salty, but she found her taste buds didn't protest. Okay, it didn't taste anything like the healthy treats she usually allowed herself.

But . . . that was okay.

Folding the note carefully, she thought back to when Liam had texted earlier about dinner, how she'd told him she would eat before she came. And he'd sent this plethora of junk food anyway. She bit her lip, dueling emotions coursing through her—touched and also exasperated.

But mostly touched.

"Oh, Liam," she whispered. "What the hell am I going to do with you?"

Mia didn't get a chance to consider the answer because the lights came on, the buzzer sounded, and the teams emerged back onto the ice. The tray remained by her feet when she rose for the anthem, but it didn't stay there.

By the time the puck was dropped, it was in her lap.

By the time Liam had his first shift, she'd made a dent in the sundae—couldn't have it melting.

And by the time the Gold cruised to victory, Liam having scored a goal and having gotten two assists, she'd finished the beer, eaten the pretzel, and consumed an ungodly amount of popcorn.

Her stomach full and feeling a bit sick from the sheer quantity of junk consumed, she cheered on the team.

Then she made her way up the stairs and to the elevators outside of Section 101.

More than a little fluff, but Mia was starting to think that perhaps some fluff might be okay.

NINE

LIAM

"Why are you in a hurry, big guy?" Brit asked, eyes assessing as she started hauling ass to the locker room. "Where are you rushing off to?"

"I'm not rushing off anywhere," he said. "Just tired."

A lie, because he *was* in a hurry.

Mia was waiting, and he'd been detained by the media. He was never interviewed after games. At this point in his career, that always happened to the other guys. Today, however, when he didn't *want* to be interviewed, when a very sexy woman was waiting for him, but he'd been pulled in anyway, he was stifling his impatience.

Thankfully, he'd managed to get through the interview quickly, even making the reporters chuckle as he gave a couple of sound bites.

Now, he needed to get his stinky ass clean and meet up with Mia.

"Does this *not* rushing have to do with the pretty Mia, who's currently keeping Mandy company in the PT Suite?"

Liam skidded to a stop and whirled around so quickly he

nearly stepped off the black mat and onto the concrete floor. The rubber protected his blades from being dulled on the cement—important during a game, less so now when the final buzzer had gone off. Still, his near-trip had done two things. One, he nearly ate it, and Brit busted a gut. Two, he'd not played it cool in any way, shape, or form, and so Brit now knew that his hurry was indeed because he was eager to meet Mia.

"Don't worry," Brit said, side-stepping him and setting her stick down in the rack outside the locker room. "I'd heard you'd asked for an escort for a guest after the game, so when I saw you'd been pulled for an interview, I made sure she was stashed away from the wolves." A wink. "Mandy will watch out for her."

"Wolves?"

"The gossip-mongers."

Liam fixed her with a look. "And that isn't you?" he asked archly.

"Rude." But Brit was grinning. "Hey, at least I fully admit to my nosy behavior," she said lightly before her face went serious. "I know it's hard to be the new one. Mandy will show her around but not scare her off. She'll be less nosy than the wives and girl-friends in the suite upstairs."

The WAGs. Shit, he hadn't thought of that.

"Technically, Mandy is a wife." A beat. "And you are, too."

"Not anymore. I'm the player. Stefan is just the ball and chain," Brit said then tapped her chin. "Hmm. I guess we need to rename the WAGs. The WHAGs? Or does that sound like some scary creature from one of those fantasy books Max is always read-ing?" She shook herself. "Not the point. Anyway, Mandy's the nicest one of us. Mia will be fine there."

Mandy *was* nice. And it was just as nice that Brit had been looking out for him and for Mia. "Thanks," he said. "You didn't have—"

She clapped him on the shoulder. "I got your back, Li." A grin. "We all do."

"You just want to know every detail along the way."

A flick of her blonde ponytail, that grin growing wider. "Damn straight. Now, get your ass in the shower"—she stepped aside, allowing him to pass by and into the locker room—"you stink."

"It's the smell of victory," he quipped.

Her amused snort trailed him into the space.

But Liam was less focused on Brit than on the woman waiting for him.

He got his gear off, showered, and fresh clothes on in record time.

———

There was a man standing very close to *his* woman.

Correction: Coop was standing very close to his woman, smiling down at her as he pointed to something in front of him.

Then Mia smiled up at him.

She smiled. At him.

He'd gotten all sharp edges and knocked on his ass, and Coop got smiles and was allowed to stand close.

Liam saw red.

He knew he was being unreasonable, but he was still irritated as he quickly closed the distance between them, sliding a hand around Mia's waist and tugging her against his side.

Her eyes shot to his, wide and with a trace of annoyance, and he knew he was lucky that she didn't knock him on his ass right then and there.

But then her face gentled, one half of her mouth curved up into a soft smile.

"Hi," she murmured.

"Hey, man." Coop clapped him on the arm. "Great game tonight."

"Hey."

Yes, Liam was a bastard because it was clipped out. Yes, he

knew he hadn't yet earned the right to be possessive. Yes, he knew he was being unreasonable.

But dammit, Coop was such a pretty boy. Even though he was married to Calle, even though they had a kid together, most women still melted under his charm. And Mia was smiling at *him*.

She glanced back down at her hands, and Liam felt a bolt of guilt.

She was holding Coop's phone, watching a video of his daughter, Emma, holding a tiny hockey stick.

"Already a natural," Mia said, handing the phone back. "She's really adorable."

"Yes, she is." Coop laughed and slipped the phone back into his pocket. "I'm biased, I know."

"We parents are allowed to be biased," Mandy said.

"It's true," Mia agreed. "I always know the good parents because they wear their pride like a badge on their sleeve."

"How many parents do you know?" Mandy asked. "By the way you say that, it sounds like a lot."

Mia shrugged. "Oh, I run a karate studio, so I meet a lot of parents."

"Wow." Pink across the trainer's cheek. "Why do I feel the urge to pull out my phone and wax poetic over my daughter just so that I know I pass muster?"

Mia laughed. "You pass." She nodded at Blane, who was holding his daughter, Madeline, and blowing raspberries on her tummy just a few tables away. "How old is she now?"

"Eighteen months."

"Old enough for me to get her into the karate studio for a real sport," Mia teased. "That one's"—she nodded at Coop, who was talking to Gabe Carter, a former M.D. and their current head trainer—"daughter has a few more months to go yet."

"You do karate for kids that small?" Mandy asked, eyes wide.

"It's more like controlled playtime for kids aged eighteen months to three years," Mia said. "But yes, they get a little karate thrown in. Mom and Ninja class meets Wednesdays and Fridays at 11:30 am."

"That sounds awesome."

"It's fun. Never without tears or chaos, but that's the age, right?" Mia smiled when a shrill cry rang out, exactly on cue. "My dad started the program, and while I think he regretted it, I like getting my baby fix."

Mandy's eyes drifted over to Blane, where he was walking their daughter, back and forth. "Dads are great." A slice of sad invaded. "Or at least, they can be."

Mia went still, and when she spoke, her voice had gentled. "Looks like your daughter has a great one."

Mandy nodded. "Maddy is lucky to have him. *I'm* lucky to—"

Max popped his head around the corner. "Ugh! So much sap in this room! Can we cool it on the love speak?" His gaze flicked to Mia. "Hi, Ms. Caldwell!"

"Hi, Max," Mia said with a smile.

Mandy shook her head, but Liam noticed the sad had faded. "You're just as bad about your *Angel*, Max Montgomery, so I don't want to hear it."

"True." Max smacked a kiss on her cheek. "See you tomorrow."

"Don't forget your stretches," she called as Max disappeared back around the corner. "How do you know Max?" she asked Mia.

"I teach his son, Brayden."

Mandy's expression softened. "Love that kid. Oh, shoot." She set down the roll of tape she held. "Excuse me for just a second," she told them, glancing over Liam's shoulder. He saw that Coop had wrapped up his conversation with Gabe and was trying to slip from the room, but Mandy didn't miss much, and her voice rang across the room, "Cooper Armstrong. A word."

"Sorry," she said in an undertone to Mia. "Herding cats."

Liam's lips twitched. "Should I be insulted?"

Mandy patted his cheek. "No, you're one of the few who actually listens to me."

"Gold star for the day," he said, lacing his fingers with Mia's. "We'll get out of your hair."

"It's no trouble," Mandy said. "I like having people around."

Mia stepped away from Liam and extended her hand. "Thanks for letting me hang with you."

"It's not too often that I meet a person who knows the difference between athletic tape and KT tape, so as far as I'm concerned, you're hired." She batted Mia's hand away. "And I don't do handshakes. I do hugs." A beat, already mid-hug when she paused. "Sorry, I should have asked if that's okay."

Mia's arms wrapped around her in turn. "It's okay. I can handle a hug."

"Just be careful," Liam said. "J.B. here is a fifth-degree black belt."

Mandy pulled back. "Really?"

A shrug. "Yeah. It comes with the territory when you're in the studio as much as I am."

"And with hard work." Liam didn't like her discounting the effort, minimizing what she could do or the commitment it took to get there. "You should see some of the kicks she can do, and the other day, she flipped me with barely any effort."

Blane chimed into the conversation. "I'm not sure I want my daughter to know that—"

"Oh, hell no," Mandy said, interrupting him. "She needs to know *all* the things. Do you teach groin shots?"

Coop, who'd drifted back over on Mandy's orders, stepped back.

Probably because she sounded positively gleeful.

Hell, Liam was having a hard time not covering himself with his hands.

"Yes," Mia said laughing, chocolate eyes filled with mirth. "We teach many different self-defense techniques."

"Great." A clap of Mandy's hand. "How do I sign up?"

"Her up," Blane said. "This is for Madeline, not you, right?"

At Mandy's considering expression, Mia laughed again, the sound settling into Liam's heart. God, he loved these people for making her laugh. "I do teach adult classes," she said. "But if we are talking about Maddy, then eighteen months is a little early for groin kicks. The rest of it, however—" She reached into her purse and pulled out a business card. "There's the studio information and my email. We can work out the details, and Maddy can have a trial class to make sure she likes it."

All the talk of groin shots aside, Liam made a mental note to send Brit a case of beer for getting Mia around Mandy. The trainer was warm and funny and made everyone feel welcome, even stubborn bastards like himself, who tended to hang on the fringes. He was starting to understand what he'd been missing by staying removed. In an attempt to protect himself when he left, he'd neglected to realize that there were good people here, ones who might become good friends.

Like Brit. Like Mandy.

Like Coop and Max and Blane.

Maybe he didn't have to be an outsider.

And Mia didn't have to be either.

He knew that he didn't want that for her. He wanted her surrounded by people who could see the soft inside, who could tease and joke. That was important for his woman, and he didn't think she'd had enough of that in her life.

And maybe thinking about someone other than himself for a change was going to help him pull his head out of his ass.

Less moping and worrying.

More living. More playing. More finding things that filled instead of deflated.

Mandy gave Mia another hug, this time without the qualifying, and then pulled back and fixed Coop in place with a glare. "Now, how are those ribs?"

"Mandy," Coop groaned.

"No fuss," she said. "Get your ass on the table and strip."

Mia glanced up at Liam, her pretty brown eyes dancing. "I like your friends."

Liam touched her cheek, knew that even a week ago, he wouldn't have considered them close enough to be friends. But it had started with Brit at practice. Hell, it had started well before that, he'd just been too closed off to see it.

Now, though, he was going to build it, strengthen it, nurture it—

Because he wasn't going to let these new connections go.

Because he wasn't going to let *Mia* go.

TEN

MIA

This was some sort of fairy tale, and she was terrified that she was going to wake up and find out it had just been a dream all along.

How else could she explain the transformation?

Liam was her fairy godmother—or father, or fairy hockey player. Hell, she didn't know. All she could do was feel.

This will all come crashing down. You'll see.

Her breath caught. The cynical words coming from the part of her that had witnessed the pieces come crashing down. First, when her mom had died. Then—

"Hey," Liam murmured. "You okay?"

Blinking, shoving down the heavy weight of all the mistakes, she just nodded and returned her gaze out the window.

"Where are we going?" she asked a few minutes later. At first, she'd thought he was driving her home, but he'd just driven past the studio. She also knew that it was a question she would have expected any of her students to ask *before* getting into a car with a person they'd only met recently, but . . . she trusted Liam, even after just a few days. Maybe it was stupid, but she had to face facts, this man was different.

She was different with him.

She felt a hundred pounds lighter. She felt like a twenty-something woman for once, instead of an old lady whose memories were heavy weights, bowing her back more and more every year.

So, Mia was just continuing on with the same vein of how she'd been proceeding all night—do as she said, not as she did.

"My condo," Liam said.

Oh, shit.

Well, clearly the do as she said, not as she did was the wrong tact.

She opened her mouth—

"We're not going to stay there," he told her, expression concerned. "Shit, I wasn't thinking how that sounded or expecting—" A sharp shake of his head. "We don't even have to go in. I just—parking is difficult around my place and—"

She relaxed.

Good man.

Liam was a good man.

Mia reached over and snagged his hand, feeling sparks at the contact, heat slide up her arm, seep into her heart. "It's fine," she said.

He blew out a breath. "I'm sorry," he told her. "I wasn't thinking. I was on post-game autopilot. There's this place nearby I always go."

"Is it a bar?" She narrowed her eyes, slid her fingers from his, and crossed her arms over her chest.

"No." Confusion dragged his brows down. "Why would I go to a bar?"

A shrug, arms dropping as relief flowed through her. "I don't know. Just seems like a very hockey player thing to do."

"What are other"—he took one hand off the steering wheel and made air quotes—"*hockey player things?*"

She knew he was teasing her, knew her words would probably

make him tease her more. But know what? She liked the teasing, and she damn well liked teasing him right back. "I don't know." A tap to her chin. "Spitting, fighting, drinking, cursing, missing teeth," she rattled off. "Stinking, beards, nice butts. Did I miss any?"

Silence.

Then he burst out laughing, taking the hand he'd made air quotes with and lacing his fingers with hers. "No," he said when he'd gained control. "I don't think you missed any. Though, I'm not sure I can be the one to realistically quantify my ass as nice or not."

She grinned. "It's nice." A light squeeze of his hand. "Better than nice in those slacks."

"That's one you missed."

"What's that?" she asked as Liam maneuvered into an underground parking spot.

"Suits," he said. "We hockey players have a lot of nice suits."

She made a face, not sure she'd call some of the suits she'd seen his teammates wearing as nice.

"Okay, so the rookies sometimes make some bad choices," he admitted.

"Which were the rookies?"

"Kelly green and sky blue."

Those were two she'd seen and winced at. "Both nice colors," she said. "Just—"

"—not on suits," they finished at the same time, sharing a grin before he pulled into a parking spot and turned off the car. "One of the best things my dad did for me was help me spend my first paycheck on nice suits."

"*All* of it?"

Liam nodded. "*All* of it. I was living at home, had no other expenses, and those five suits we had made are still with me in my rotation seven years later. One navy, two gray, a black, and a brown." He grinned. "No Kelly green in sight."

She chuckled and unhooked her seat belt. "Maybe not the

most prudent financial decision for a first paycheck, but I can understand the need."

"Me, too." He unbuckled then reached into the back seat for his bag. "Especially since I wanted to dump all my money into a nice car."

Since she was sitting in a very sleek, nice car, she asked, "How long did that take?"

"Oh, ages," he said and opened his door. "All the way until my third paycheck."

Mia laughed as she pushed out of the passenger's seat. "What did you use the second for?"

"First and last month's rent, plus a security deposit on my first place."

"How old were you?"

He rounded the car and took her hand, bleeping the car locks and leading her to a set of stairs. True to form, he didn't take her up to his condo. Instead the stairs led to a lobby, and they walked over to a set of large glass doors. "Eighteen," he said. "I was drafted and had the choice for college or straight into the pros. I chose hockey. I loved it, wanted as much time with the sport as I could."

"So young," she said. "Is that why—?" She cut off the question she'd been about to ask.

Liam had just held the door so she could walk out. When she stopped herself, he frowned, slipped through the opening, and took her hand. "Is that why . . .?" he prompted.

"No," she said. "It's a stupid question."

He crowded her, just turned and crowded her against the wall of the building, one hand going to her waist, the other to her cheek. "What, Mia?"

Any other man crowding her like this, and he'd be on his ass.

This man.

She caved.

"What kinds of suits did you buy after the first round?"

Well, partly caved because while she asked *a* question, it wasn't the question she'd planned on asking.

Which Liam knew.

Because while he grinned and said, "Several plaids, a pinstripe, and even a paisley," his eyes never left hers. He bent until his mouth was a hairsbreadth away, his hot breaths puffing against her lips. This man made her want . . . so many things she'd never allowed her brain to even contemplate, let alone hope for. "Fuck, you're gorgeous," he said, shifting closer, his lips brushing hers as he spoke in that roughened velvet of his voice, the one that dripped down her stomach, rolling in a trail of hot, liquid honey.

Straight to her pussy.

"Fuck," he growled. "What put that expression on your face, J.B.?"

Yeah, no. Not sharing with the class.

He smirked, the hand on her waist sliding down, slipping in an inch.

Her breath caught.

"What question were you going to ask?" The hand on her neck slid up and down, tracing light patterns on her skin and making her shiver.

It also loosened her tongue.

"I was going to ask if that was why you were sad about your contract maybe not getting renewed," she said softly, gently, because she didn't want to hurt this man. "If it's because you love the game so much and you're worried that losing it will . . ."

She trailed off, not sure how to finish the thought.

Liam was quiet for a while, eyes not leaving hers, the stormy pools made darker by the moonlight. Then he shifted slightly, stopped crowding her. For a minute, her heart skipped a beat, stomach sinking, thinking he was retreating. But then he slid his hand from her waist to her shoulders and tugged her against his side.

"I do love the game," he said, starting to walk again, taking her alongside him. "But my sadness came not from losing the game—

or at least not *solely* losing it. These last years in the league have been tough. I had a three-year contract when I was initially signed. Now, I've been with four teams in as many years, shuffled around more for better trade picks than because I was a hot commodity." He sighed. "I started to hate playing. Hated the games, the practices, the competition. My teammates, my coaches. I despised the whole process." A shrug that slid his side along hers, that lifted goose bumps on her skin, but she was too intrigued by this man, worried about the shadows in his eyes to do more than obliquely acknowledge that the attraction between them never seemed to dissipate. It only grew larger, wound tighter, burned hotter.

Only *this* was more important.

His words. His expression. His body language.

All told her that she could ask him anything and he would tell her.

"Why?" she asked. "What happened?"

He sighed, and she wrapped her arm around his waist, holding him tightly and wanting to take the flare of pain in his eyes away. She could take it. She'd dealt with plenty of pain in her life. Her spine was strong, her shoulders capable of hefting the extra burden.

"It would be easier if I could pinpoint one thing," he said. "But it was such a combination of factors. I had a really difficult coach at my first team. He was a screamer, and his technique was to break players down in order to build them back up." Another sigh. "Maybe that would work with some guys. With me, knowing that after every game I would have a meeting highlighting my errors then have homework to watch multiple videos breaking down every single thing I did wrong during a game—from a missed stride to a bobbled puck to a legitimate issue with my play that needed to be addressed—well, it wreaked havoc with my confidence."

"That sounds like a lot at once."

"Yeah," he said. "But look, I'm from a family of hockey players. My brothers, my dad, my grandfather were all in the league.

I'd had tough coaching my whole life. I should have been able to handle it."

Something clicked in her mind. "Like *they* handled it."

"Yes."

"How good are they?" she asked. "I started watching hockey when we got the Gold, mostly because my dad was into it. I know our team, but I'm not familiar with many players from the others."

He tugged her to the right, down a darkened alley that would normally have her dragging her heels and refusing to go. But she was familiar with this neighborhood, so close to where she'd grown up, and had an inkling where he was leading her.

"Dad and Grandpa are in the Hall of Fame. My older brother Laich is probably going to be in next year, and Luke as soon as enough years have passed."

"So, they were good."

"Yeah."

"And you're struggling."

Silence, then, "Yeah."

"What happened after the first contract?"

"I got traded. Coach was better. Team was not."

Shit.

"Rinse. Repeat two more times. Except, the middle two were terrible. Decent coaches and teammates, but my family was in preservation mode. I'd get off the ice and my cell would be filled with messages." His fingers clenched then released on her hip. "I should be grateful. They called because they cared. They knew I was talented, wanted to help me find the potential."

"But it only made things worse."

"Yeah," he whispered, and she let her eyes go to the street, the gray, almost colorless walls at this time of night of the buildings on either side of the alley. Mia flicked her gaze to the sky, the moon, not wanting to see the bleakness in his own gaze. "It was worse. I was imploding. Fourth line, if I was lucky. Scratched from the roster almost as much as I played. Some of the guys who were battling injuries got more ice time than I did." He sighed. "I just couldn't get out of my head."

"And now?"

"I couldn't understand why the Gold picked me up. Couldn't fathom that a team who'd won the Cup for two out of the last three years would want me."

"But they did."

"Yeah," he said, leading them out of the alley and up a hill to the right. More rule-bending, as she knew this trail was not open at almost midnight, but she didn't falter this time, didn't drag her heels.

Instead, she continued trying to unravel the pain inside this man. "It seemed like you found something tonight."

"Brit," he said.

Mia tilted her head up in question. Liam bent, brushed his mouth over hers.

"She cornered me at practice the other day, roped me into a killer workout," he said. "But more than the running, she reminded me what a team could be like. Along with Blane, and Max, and Coop."

"Friends."

"Yeah," he said. "And you saw what Mandy is like. It's almost impossible to not feel included. Add in coaching that is quality without yelling and tearing down, and . . . I guess I'm starting to feel like myself again."

"And you're in love."

He froze, stared down out her with his jaw fallen open.

She processed her words, felt a cold sweat break out on her neck. "I meant with the game again," she quickly added.

Silence then, "Yeah, of course."

Her cheeks were hot, but thankfully the darkness hid the flush. "So, hockey is getting a little better."

He nodded. "It is. I feel like I'm finding the enjoyment, like I can make a place here."

"Your game seems to speak to that."

"I'm just going to keep my head down and keep working. Push through the insecurities and grab on to the opportunity in front of me." Another nod, decisive this time. "Even if this does turn out to be my last season, I'm going to make the most of it."

"I'm proud of you."

His breath caught.

"I know we're just getting to know each other," she murmured. "I know it probably doesn't mean much, but I think it's admirable that you're pushing through. It's not easy."

He stopped again, gaze unfathomable, but his hand when it brushed her cheek, was warm. Gentle.

"It means a lot, J.B.," he whispered. "A lot."

Then he was kissing her. Or maybe she was kissing him.

Mia didn't know, and she didn't care. She reveled in the feel of his strong shoulders beneath her hands, the hard breadth of his chest pressing against hers, the way his tongue brushed alongside hers with gentle strokes, his fingers clenching on her waist, his body so hot and heady and intoxicating.

She was drunk on this man and his kisses.

"You know you're once again getting me to break rules I would never allow my students to," she said when they finally broke apart to breathe in some much-needed oxygen. She rested her palm over his heart, concentrated on slowing her inhalations and exhalations.

In. Out. In. Out. Slow. Steady.

Do *not* think about the moisture pooling between her thighs, nor the need that was twisting her insides. She might forget about breaking rules and start breaking *laws*—indecent exposure ones.

"I have no idea what you're talking about," he said innocently, his pulse thundering against her palm.

Way *too* innocently.

"Kite Hill isn't open this late," she said, walking forward, tugging *him* this time.

"Actually—" He twisted in front of her, and she skidded to a stop, her chest flush to his. Not that she was complaining, especially when he punctuated the action by slanting his mouth across hers and kissing her until her lungs screamed for oxygen.

"Actually," he repeated when they broke apart, threading their fingers together and walking forward with her again. "Kite Hill is open until midnight."

Mia glanced down at her watch. "It's 11:52."

"Technically not breaking the rules."

Shaking her head, she walked beside him up the short incline, breath catching not from the exertion, but from the view at the top—and maybe *also* from this man. This man, who had a sensitive heart. This man, who wanted so badly to do his best. To make his family proud. To find his place.

This troublesome, rule-breaking man who'd managed to weasel his way into *her* heart.

"Come here," he said, voice deeper, huskier, and she turned from the view to see that he'd pulled a blanket from his bag and spread it on the ground.

Mia went to him.

This was a fairy tale that was probably going to implode, but she found she couldn't resist it, couldn't resist him.

She crossed the grass on quiet feet, let him tug her down onto his lap.

"You know what else helped me clear the fog enough to start moving forward again?" He stroked a hand down her ponytail, brushing her nape, making her shiver. "Or rather who?"

She shook her head. "No."

"You."

Twisting, she glanced up at him. "Me?" she asked, incredulous.

"Don't think I forgot that you saved my life, J.B.," he said, tugging lightly at her hair. "I was in that street thinking morose, pathetic thoughts. Considering that everything might be over, and I should put my math degree to good use—"

"You have a math degree?"

The ghost of a smile before his lips pressed to hers for a short but blazing kiss. "Not the point in this conversation," he teased. "But yes, I actually have two degrees in math, a bachelor's and a master's."

"Smart."

A flash of white teeth. "Occasionally."

"Li—"

"Shh," he said, tugging her back against his chest. "I'm trying to tell you something important."

"Fine," she muttered, wanting to know more about how he'd gotten those degrees, but also not wanting to stop him from telling her what he felt like he needed to say.

"I was in the street. In my head. So fucking twisted up, and I just thought . . . *enough*." Her throat went tight. "And then this tough, strong angel flew in out of nowhere and yanked me out of harm's way." He ran his hand up and down her arm. "You saved me, knocked some fucking sense into this hard-ass head. And . . . after seeing you, teasing you, touching and kissing and talking with you, I started feeling more like myself than I had in years." He cupped her cheek. "You make me feel like it's okay to just be me. No reservations. No holding back. No . . . fear."

Pulse pounding, she spun in his hold, wrapped her arms around his neck, and held him tight.

That was what he did for her.

Cleared the armor away. Made her think of all the possibilities. Made her hope and believe that things might actually be okay. That she might deserve some happy, some fluff.

She wanted to tell him that.

To confess what she'd done. To get it off her chest, relieve the burden she carried around.

God, she wanted that *so* fucking intensely, to the point that it was nearly impossible to quell the words.

But . . . this was Liam's moment.

He'd done so much for her already, helped her see the possibilities, to have fun, to feel hope again. Tonight could be just about him. Another time could be about her.

She just prayed that they would have another time.

Because as much as she hoped, reality wasn't so easy to shed.

Liam might be traded. Or not have his contract renewed and move away to use those math degrees.

Liam might stop looking at her like he was tonight.

The fog had cleared, and he might realize exactly how much he deserved, this good man, this sweet man, this sensitive man.

So yeah, another time could be about Mia.

Tonight, she wanted to soak in this feeling, to hold it close, tuck it someplace safe.

And she wanted him to laugh. To feel light and buoyant. To give him some of the joy and fluff he'd given her.

Leaning back, she dropped her lips so they were very close to his.

"Liam?"

"Hmm?" he asked, eyes dilating, hands tracing the curves of her waist, her hips, her ass.

"I think you just like me because I can do this."

And then she *moved*—flipping them in a Jujitsu move that had her on top one moment, him on top the next. Her legs parted and his pelvis slipped between her thighs, moving forward to brush the hardening length of his cock against her pussy.

Layers and layers of clothes between them.

Yet, it still was the single most erotic moment of her life, seeing Liam braced over her, watching his face go hungry, feeling his erection against her.

"You're so fucking beautiful," he whispered.

Then he kissed her.

Under the moonlight, the stars overhead, the lights of the buildings around them filling the night sky, his body pressed to hers so that she could feel his heart beating as rapidly as her own.

He kissed her.

He sliced through all the toughness she used to protect herself, wove himself right into the very marrow of her bones.

And Mia knew she would never be the same.

Especially, when she could hardly summon a worry after they finally managed to pull apart, after Liam stowed the blanket away, after they made their way down the hill . . . even though making their way down was completed well after midnight.

A broken rule meant nothing.

Because she had this man.

ELEVEN

LIAM

The woman was brilliant, even cradling a sleeping baby on her shoulder.

Calle drew a line on the whiteboard he was holding because as brilliant and capable as the Gold's assistant coach—her focus on offense—was, she still only had two hands.

"So," she said, pairing the drawing with words, "if you slide this way on the face-off against the Ducks, you'll draw the D enough to let Blue win the puck forward and have a lane to the net."

Liam nodded. "Yeah. I can do that for sure."

But his mind was spinning, because he wasn't on a line with Blue and Coop. He wasn't *on* the top line.

He hadn't been on the first line since his inaugural season . . . and that had quickly changed.

"If you come to the optional skate in the morning," she said, capping the pen in a move that was surprisingly natural given that she'd only used one hand. But then again, she was a mom, and moms had superpowers. "Coop and Blue will be there for us to run it through."

"I'll be there," he said, having been planning on it anyway. "Am I—" He stopped himself. A player didn't ask where he was going to play. He shut up and played where he was told. "Thanks for the suggestion," he said. "I'll get it down."

"I know you will."

He turned and started heading for the showers. Practice was done, and he'd been planning on some off-ice training, a massage, a shower, and then . . . counting down the minutes until he could see Mia that night for the movie. What he *hadn't* been planning on was being stopped by a coach in the hall, and thus, hadn't been able to prevent his stomach from twisting itself into knots with nervous energy.

"Liam." Calle's voice halted him a couple of steps away.

He turned back. "Yeah, Coach?"

She opened her mouth, closed it, and seemed to debate something for a long moment. Then she stepped closer and said, "You'll be on that top line because that's where you belong. You, Coop, and Blue have chemistry. We saw that in the power play last night, at practice this morning." Her baby, Emma, fussed quietly, and Calle shifted her, rocking back and forth slightly as she spoke. "You're not there because of a name or because of any history. You're there because you're the right fit at this time. Nothing more. Nothing less."

Liam swallowed hard, nodded. "Okay, Coach."

Blue eyes on his for a long moment before a small smile curved her lips, but before she could say anything further, Emma let out a squawk that was loud enough to make Liam jump. "This one is hungry, apparently," she told him. "I'll see you in the morning."

He waved as she disappeared down the hall, Calle's transition from hockey coach to mom somehow instant but not jarring. It was seamless. It was her. It was effortless, and Liam found himself soaking in some of that smooth shifting, that calm confidence. It seeped through his skin, sank into his bones, and instead of being terrified about being in that top spot, he found he was looking forward to it.

Calle was right.

They did have chemistry, and it had been fun as hell to be on the power play with those two last night, being able to move and shift and pass and shoot, while knowing instinctively where they would be. He'd had to look, of course. There weren't too many spaces in the NHL where someone could make a blind pass without having it get picked off. But Liam had found he'd been able to look out of the corner of his eye, or with simply a quick glance. He hadn't had to spend too much time searching, and that had freed up even more time and space.

They'd controlled the puck. The ice.

They'd been patient—despite the fans screaming, "Shoot it!" in the stands.

Though they'd eventually shot . . . and scored.

Liam had received the second assist, having passed it to Coop, who'd passed it to Blue, who'd then actually put the puck into the net. But it might as well have been him who'd scored the goal.

Because it had been really fucking fun.

Blinking, thinking that Blane had been speaking more than a little bit of truth the other day in the locker room when telling him they all played better when it was a more relaxed environment, Liam got his ass in gear.

He was the last player near the ice, but not on it, everyone else having already scattered to address individual needs. Some, like Brit, were still out there, getting a bit more practice in. Others would head to the weight room or PT for therapy. He was heading to the off-ice space—more resistance bands and jump boxes than dumbbells and weight benches. Liam was strong. He'd been hitting the weights a lot over the last few years, thinking that he needed to bulk up, but after having seen lithe Mia moving the other day, he was thinking that agile, flexible muscle was the way to go.

Strength, of course.

But flexibility for explosive bursts of speed and quick changes in direction.

That had always been in his wheelhouse, so why had he spent so much time trying to turn his body into something it wasn't?

Because Williamsons were big. They were brawn. They finished checks and bodied players off the puck.

Except, that wasn't him.

He waited for the disappointment to hit him as he walked down the hall, waited for that old bleakness to take hold. Only this time, it didn't. Instead, he was more at peace than he'd been in a long time.

This was him.

That was fine.

He dropped his gloves in the bin the equipment manager had left out, turned and stepped into the locker room. Then—

"Oof!"

The balled-up sock hit him right in the face.

Max was grinning, the bastard.

"I hope that was clean, fucker," Liam grumbled, picking up the sock and launching it back.

"Now, come on, man," Max said, dodging it. "You know me better than that."

Unfortunately, Liam did . . . or well, at least, he'd felt the amount of sweat in the sock when he'd picked it up to throw it at his teammate.

Fucking gross.

But then again . . . hockey.

Shaking his head, he laughed when Coop came in behind him, saying, "Give Liam a break. He hasn't had to deal with your stinky ass feet as long as the rest of us."

Max yanked off his other skate. "Well, at least I don't have a stinky a—"

"Gentlemen," Brit scolded, striding into the room, her helmet propped up on her head. "Bad mannered, all of you. Why can't you—*hey!*"

Blane had thrown *his* sock at her.

She threw it back, clocking Blue across the cheek.

And thus began the Gold Sock War. Spoken about for generations to come.

Or not.

Rather, Liam joined in with the rest of the guys fucking around, dodging and ducking dirty socks and the odd glove and elbow pad, laughing like an idiot when he nailed Max right on the chin.

It was just stupid fun.

But it was more fun than Liam had had with his teammates in years.

And he felt another piece of himself slide back into place.

This was . . . right.

———

"I'll talk to him, sweetheart," his mother, Fran, said later that afternoon. "I think it's time to pull out the brass balls and steel wool."

Liam snorted, knowing that was his only hope at de-escalating his father's campaign at this point. He'd tried texting his dad back, saying thanks for the advice, but he needed some space. He'd said he was going to take this time to listen to his coaches, to learn the Gold's system.

That had gone over . . .

About as well as too-soft ice.

Sluggish and pissing the players—or former players, in his dad's case—off.

He'd gotten several voicemails in addition to the text, all in the vein of helping, though with tightly contained fury, as though his dad couldn't believe Liam didn't want his help.

So, he'd called. He'd spoken to his father, tried to explain it wasn't that at all. He always appreciated the thought, the help, but that he needed to get out of his own head.

To which his dad had taken to mean Liam had just needed tips on the Gold's offensive system, tips his dad had gathered from watching tapes.

Tapes.

His dad was studying hockey like he was playing it.

For Liam.

Which was a nice gesture, really, he got that.

But it was . . . too fucking much.

Hence, the big guns.

Moms and their superpowers.

"I love you, guys," he told his mom. "But I'm already trying to adjust, and it's hard when dad is texting me every hour."

"I know, Li." She sighed. "I'm sorry, babes. I'll talk to him."

"Thanks, Mom."

A pause. "I wonder if I can put parental controls on his phone?"

Liam laughed but half-considered the idea for a second before discounting it. "He'd probably be on the next plane out here if you did."

"There is that." She sighed again. "I'll get him straightened out," she promised. "Now, tell me. How do you like San Francisco? It's been years since I've been there."

They spent a few minutes chatting about the weather—positively balmy when compared to Buffalo, where his parents lived—and the tourist sites his mom wanted to see when they were able to schedule a trip out—probably in a couple of months, since Laich's wife was pregnant and his mom was on babysitting duty.

It felt nice to catch up on the banal things.

"Have you met anyone special out there?" she asked just before they hung up.

It felt even nicer to be able to answer that question with—

"Yes, Mom. And she's great." He leaned back on his couch and grinned. "Now I have to convince her I'm just as great."

His mom laughed. "Well, babes, I can't wait to meet her," she said. "Because I know that won't take you long."

"You have to say that. You're my mom."

"Yes, I do." A beat. "But it's also true."

He'd scoffed, but his heart had been full by the time they hung up.

And best part of that conversation? Aside from the ego boost of his mom saying he was great?

The text messages and voicemails from his dad stopped.

———

"I can't believe I'm at the movies and not eating popcorn," he grumbled, partly because the movie theater popcorn smelled amazeballs, permeating the air around them until he could almost tangibly grab on to it, but mostly because he wanted to see what Mia would say.

She didn't disappoint.

Shifting in the seat next to him—armrest up, thanks to his bit of sneaky . . . but also probably because she allowed it to stay up— she reached into her purse.

"Here," she snapped, smacking him in the chest with a bag.

At first, Liam thought she'd brought popcorn.

Then he glanced down and nearly busted a gut.

"Carrot sticks?" he exclaimed.

A roll of her pretty brown eyes. "Yes," she said primly. "And you don't have to say it like *that*. Carrot sticks are delicious, low calorie, and I believe they fit in quite nicely with your plant-based meal plan, if what you were telling me about it was the truth."

He glared down at the carrots.

Cruelty. That was what the carrots were. Delicious, buttery, freshly popped popcorn all around him, and he had carrots. "I was telling the truth," he muttered.

"Good," she said. "I like it when people are honest." A beat. "Now, eat the bloody carrots."

"Appetizing," he said darkly, but on purpose, because he knew when she heard she would turn to glare at him, and that the action would bring her lips very close to his.

"I—"

He kissed her, tasted her outrage on his tongue, soothed it with teasing sips, gentle strokes, letting her know he'd only been playing. No words, only touch. Only the two of them and their bodies, their mouths, their mingled breaths.

Her hand was against his chest, resting on the spot over his heart, probably able to feel how rapidly the organ was beating.

Because of this woman.

Because of the soft and hard.

Because of the—

"Ow!" he exclaimed, leaning back, hand coming up to his bottom lip, which she had nipped with enough pressure to sting.

"That's for teasing me," she said with a glare, and then she surprised him by taking his mouth in a hot, slow kiss that had his cock going hard and his brain threatening to melt and leak out through his ears.

"What was that for?" he asked when they broke away, his lungs sawing.

"For teasing me." A coy smile curved her lips, making him want to kiss her again, to forget about the fact they were at the movies at all, and to—

Fuck it. He kissed her again.

"What was *that* for?" she asked this time, her mouth swollen and tinged with red. Her eyes were heavy-lidded, and Liam couldn't help but wonder if they would get even heavier after he made her come.

"That"—he rubbed his thumb lightly back and forth over her bottom lip—"was a thank you for the carrots."

She snorted, and he really deserved another smack across the chest from the bag of orange veggie sticks. Instead, as usual, she surprised him. Mia slid a little closer and rested her head against his shoulder, soft and sweet. But her words, when they came, were tart, just like he preferred.

"Just shut up and eat the damn carrots."

The lights overhead had gone dim. The first preview was cueing up on the screen. He didn't like people who talked during the movies—and that included the previews.

But that wasn't why Liam shut up, why he ate the *damn* carrots.

He shut up, he ate the carrots because Mia had given them to him. Because she'd thought ahead enough to know he might get hungry, because she'd brought him a snack that he could eat and keep on the meal plan.

She was taking care of him.

In her own way. In the perfect, most thoughtful way.

So much soft inside that hard exterior.

Liam shut up and ate them because he knew how lucky he was to have the gift of Mia revealing that softness to him.

And because he wasn't going to squander it.

But . . . he still got the final word in. He reached into his pocket and pulled out the bar of dark chocolate. One that Nutritionist Rebecca recommended because it was high in cacao and didn't have any added sugars.

In fact, it was the one sweet they were allowed to eat on non-cheat days.

But Liam hadn't brought it for himself.

He handed it to Mia, nipped her ear when she tried to refuse and hand it back.

And then he smiled when she opened the wrapper with a sigh before proceeding to eat every last bite.

She might be taking care of him, but he'd be damned if he didn't take care of her right back.

TWELVE

MIA

She wasn't sitting on the glass this time, but still the view was pretty damned good.

Maybe even better than being in the front row.

Because higher up, she could see more of the ice, really bear witness to how fast the guys were.

Max skated up the boards, crashing into a player from the opposing team with enough force to make Mia wince and struggle to recognize the funny, laidback troublemaker who'd attended so many of Brayden's classes and belt promotions over the years with this intense, brute who apparently didn't have any qualms with laying out his opponents.

She watched as he merely straightened his helmet in a quick move then continued skating into the other team's zone, her eyes struggling to compartmentalize every detail on the ice.

Look, she'd been to games previously.

Once, after the team had begun their inaugural season, sitting way up in the top row. Twice in a box, a Christmas present from Max and his family.

But she'd never been as invested in the games as tonight, as the previous time she was here. Because . . . she was here for Liam. Because she watched his every shift with kind of a nervous energy, wanting him to do well, wincing when he got checked, breath catching when he skated down for the offense. She was taking in the whole team, sure, but she wasn't rooting for the whole team, at least not like she was rooting for Liam.

His confidence was growing play by play. Even just newly knowing him, Mia could see that much, just as she saw the joy, the determination on his face every time he was on the ice.

And watching him skate with Blue and Coop was something special.

It was almost like they were an extension of each other, moving in unison, no fumbles, constantly rotating, shifting, changing around until the other team struggled to keep an eye on them.

By the time the third period rolled around, Liam's line had already scored three times. One from Blue, two from Coop, Liam assisting on all three.

Watching his smile, huge and proud when he'd skated over to high five Coop after the winger's second goal, made her heart swell.

Good man.

You don't let a good man go.

The thought, in her mother's voice, came so far out of left field that Mia almost felt the words like a physical slap.

God, it had been so long since she'd thought about her mom.

Usually, all of her guilt centered around her dad, around what had happened after. Typically, she was able to forget the painful events that had led up to everything after because she had so many regrets about hurting the man who had been the center of her universe.

Tonight . . . was different.

She couldn't not look at those men on the ice. Fearless, strong, brave, and not remember that her mom had been like that once.

Everyone who had known her and her father through the

studio thought that she inherited her strength from him—and Mia supposed she *had* in a way. Her dad had continued on after they had lost her mother, had invested blood, sweat, and tears into the studio, the programs that had been her mother's, his wife's dream.

But his strength was a quiet steadiness.

Enduring like the ocean's waves eroding a beach or a river cutting through stone over thousands of years.

Stark. Harsh. Cutting down, pulling apart, reducing to pieces.

He'd been the perfect complement to her mom.

She was confidence and the blasting heat of the sun. She was lightning, the boom of thunder, an earthquake forming a huge crack in the crust of the planet.

Fearless. Quick. Burned hot, hotter than any other person Mia had ever met.

Ying and Yang. Two opposite sides of the coin. *All* the clichés.

But what she remembered most was how her mother's hot had tempered her father's cold, how the pieces had been rebuilt after they'd been taken apart, how the sharp and quick had been interspaced with slow and enduring.

Once she'd had everything.

After . . . she'd only had erosion.

After, she had guilt. Her own special brand that paired with her father's derision had shattered her totally, and she'd been reformed, any of that lightning in a bottle she might have inherited from her mother shoved deep down because her father couldn't bear to see it.

No more adventures. Everything was carefully controlled.

No more pushing the limits because she'd destroyed them with her selfishness.

No more fluff or extras or asking for something she didn't decidedly earn on her own. Those urges, those needs, had to be buried away because her father couldn't tolerate her asking or begging or wanting something.

Because her wanting, her begging, her asking had changed *everything*.

The sharp trill of multiple whistles drew her eyes to the ice, had her focusing on the game rather than the bleak thoughts and sad memories blaring through her mind.

She glanced up to a scrum in front of the Gold's net, one of the players from the other team bumping into Brit. Liam got between them, pushing back the asshole who was taking a cheap shot at Brit well after the whistle. Mia had watched enough hockey to be pissed that he'd dared to touch their goalie and cheered when Liam gave the fucker a hard shove. Unfortunately, the player was a good six inches taller and had probably twenty pounds on Liam. He shoved back hard, and Liam fell, landing ass first on the ice.

Mia winced, but he was on his feet in an instant, launching himself at the player who'd knocked him down, but Max had already gotten there, had the asshole in a headlock.

Brit meanwhile had calmly grabbed her water bottle and skated away from the mess . . . though Mia did see the other woman share a little love tap to the opposing player's cup.

Mia chuckled.

Sneaky. She liked it.

She liked even more the fact that Liam didn't back down from the physicality, that he was as perseverant as a pit bull but didn't seem upset that the bigger, and presumably stronger, Max had stepped in.

Liam just grinned, fist-bumped his teammate, and then skated to the bench, the whole episode more about protecting their goalie and the other team's frustration to not be getting any sort of offense going, rather than an intent to injure or something that would result in penalties.

There were, however, plenty of f-bombs, Mia thought, reading Liam's lips as he made his way to the bench, chirping at the player who'd hit Brit.

This was a different side of him to witness, but she found she liked the fire.

Then he glanced up, seeming to pick her out of the hundreds of other people in her section. His gray eyes stared intently into hers, and the smile he sent her way? Well, that hot, sexy as shit smirk warmed her from her head to her toes.

The last of the painful tenterhooks of her past slid away.

The man had kissed her on the studio doorstep the night before, refusing to come in, to come up for a glass of water—no beer on non-Cheat Days, either. He'd said he owed her one date where he didn't break any rules.

That had made her frown and ask, "What rule could you possibly be breaking by coming inside?"

To which he'd bent very close, the heat of his chest against hers, his hot breath in her ear, raising goose bumps on her skin, and then he'd said, "Because if I come inside, I'm going to be coming *inside*, J.B., and I think that's illegal with these plate glass windows overlooking the street."

Probably the line should have pissed her off. He'd made an assumption about what she was offering.

But Mia would have been lying if she'd said she *hadn't* been offering to let him inside—her body that was.

Also, ew.

That was way too much inside talk for this time of the evening.

Was there ever a good time—?

She shook her head sharply. God, she was as bad as him, except Liam's innuendos sounded a hell of a lot sexier when breathed in her ear in that rasped velvet voice rather than the dirty thoughts in her mind.

Rolling her eyes at herself, she knew that innuendo or not, she wanted Liam.

It was probably too soon. But then again, that was her mantra when it came to Liam. Even though it was exactly what her father had cautioned her against time and again. *Don't want too much. Don't expect more than you're given. Don't need another person.*

She'd spent the ten years since her mother had died grasping on to that lesson, trying to ease her dad's pain, to realize his dreams, and in turn, her mother's dreams.

Closed down. Locked up. Safe. Secure.

The part she'd missed was what had remained unspoken by her father, but what was still very much there. *Don't need another person . . . so much that it will eviscerate you when they're gone.*

Yet, she'd still wanted that, still yearned, still needed.

Only, she hadn't known that until Liam had shoved open the door.

And fuck, how she wanted.

Him. Her. In bed. On Kite Hill. At the movies. In her studio cleaning fucking mats.

He'd told her that when he looked into her eyes, he saw himself.

Well, when she looked into his, she finally felt like she could breathe.

Probably, that should have terrified her—how much she wanted, how much this man made her feel. But he'd opened the door, and Mia was feeling more and more like the Mia of old. More and more like the Mini-Maura, as she'd often been called growing up.

A spitting image of her mom.

A near-replica in personality.

Quick to laugh. A streak of mischievousness a mile wide. Easy laughter. Intense drive and a work ethic that would put most people on the planet to shame.

Only the last two had remained on the surface over the decade since her mother had died.

Now, the rest of those traits were bubbling up, seeping through cracks in the steel surrounding her, keeping her safe. She found she really liked teasing Liam, found she could laugh when he was nearby . . . and when he wasn't. Mia was herself again, really truly herself for the first time since the day she'd turned sixteen.

Since the day everything in her life had changed.

The buzzer sounded, signaling the end of the game, and she stood, the past slipping back down, her eagerness to see Liam overtaking the shadows of her memories. She shuffled her way up the stairs, slowly made the trek around the concourse until she arrived at a familiar bank of elevators and saw the smiling brunette standing there.

"Mia!" Mandy called, waving wildly.

"Hi," Mia waved back, pushed her way through the crowd.

"Great game," Mandy said, swiping her card and preceding her onto the elevator.

"It was really fun to watch," Mia agreed.

Mandy nodded, practically bouncing on her toes. "And no one got hurt. Oh! Did you see that play with . . ." She trailed off, talking about something along one of the goal lines, and while Mia was happy to see the other woman, wanted to get to know her better, if she was being honest, she wanted to see Liam more.

That sexy smile.

That joy on his face when he'd played.

Her mom was in her heart, encouraging her forward, whispering to let the steel go completely.

To give in to the want, the need.

The thought of what giving in might mean had Mia's pulse pounding in her veins, her breathing coming faster.

Then the elevator doors opened, and she saw Liam standing there.

Hell, who needed to breathe?

She launched herself out of the metal car and into his arms.

His mouth collided with hers, and the rest of the world fell away.

Thirteen

"Not fair, J.B.," he murmured, setting Mia back on her feet after the kiss that had threatened to scorch his eyebrows.

"What?" she said, fingers tightening on his shoulders.

"There are too many people around for me to kiss you the way I want to."

That cleared some of the fog in her eyes, and Mia's cheeks flared red. He caught a glimpse of Mandy shamelessly watching them, a shit-eating smirk on her lips, and Liam knew this bit of news would be on the gossip train in a matter of moments.

In fact, if the sly smile as Mandy slipped her cell into her pocket was any indication, Mia's launching act had been captured on film.

He paused, wondered how much he'd need to pay to get that picture.

Not to delete, but to frame on his wall.

Because something in Mia had changed . . . and it had shifted things between them.

From the moment he'd met her, Liam had been drawn to

Mia, as though there was a filament connecting them, sewing them together from the instant she'd pulled him out of the path of that car. It had been growing, strengthening, transforming gossamer threads into a thin, but sturdy cotton. He might have even said it was working its way toward rope or nylon, or was it silk that supposed to be the strongest? Or perhaps that was denim?

Or maybe this line of thinking was useless because today had bypassed fabric altogether.

Steel.

The connection had hardened into metal because she was . . . open.

Lighter. That fluff peeking through.

"Don't worry, J.B.," he murmured and kissed her again, even though he was sweaty and still in his gear, even though he was still wearing his skates and had to bend a good number of inches to take her lips. "I liked it," he said, pulling back. "Come on. I'll change really quick, and we can go out and break some more rules."

"Just because I kissed you doesn't mean that we're not going to follow the rules."

A pert response that went straight to his cock.

Okay, just one more.

Liam kissed her until his lungs screamed for air, until he was breathing more heavily than after a long-ass shift on the ice.

Only then did he step back and take her hand.

"Sorry," he whispered. "I couldn't help myself." He brushed a hand down her arm. "I should have at least showered first."

Mia's pupils were darkened, widened until the black almost eclipsed the chocolate brown. The weight of those eyes, of her gaze was heavy as it traced down his body and back up. "No, you shouldn't have." White teeth pressing into her bottom lip. "You definitely shouldn't have."

His cock, half-mast from the kiss, went fully hard—and it wasn't exactly comfortable in his cup.

He tried shifting it surreptitiously, but this woman didn't miss anything.

"Problem?" she asked, lifting a brow.

"Yeah," he muttered, nipping at her earlobe. "And you know exactly why."

Hands on his chest, fingers digging into the front of his shoulder pads for a moment before she pushed him away. "Go," she whispered. "Do what you need to do." A beat. "I'll think about breaking the rules."

He winced when his cock twitched, liking that idea a whole hell of a lot.

Mia saw, giggling as she stepped away, and walked over to Mandy with total calm, as though she and Liam hadn't been in their own personal bubble of want and need and desire.

"Are you sure I won't be bugging you, if I hang out?" he heard her ask.

Mandy linked her arm through Mia's. "Nope. I'll put you to work." She waved her fingers over her shoulder in Liam's direction. "Plus, I get all the gossip on you and tall, stubbled, and talented over there. The girls have so many questions. I promised them I'd bring you up to the Family Suite in a bit."

His stomach knotted.

No, he'd deliberately been avoiding bringing Mia to the Family Suite to meet the wives and girlfriends.

Because he knew that they were the other half of the gossip train.

Overwhelming, meant well, but . . . still a *lot*.

He opened his mouth to say . . . something, but unfortunately nothing came to mind.

Mia, as she often seemed to do, beat him to the punch.

Her gaze flicked over her shoulder, and she smiled at him.

A different smile, no sharp in sight. It was straight cotton candy, floating through the space between them and dissolving the moment it touched his skin. But it didn't disappear. It coated him with sweetness.

Unexpected, that tart tempered with sweet. But then again, when was this woman anything but unexpected?

Swooping in out of nowhere to save him.

Knocking him to his ass more than once.

Carrot sticks at the movies.

Scorching kisses outside of elevators.

A gentle look that told him to take his time, that she'd be fine.

As he watched her disappear down the hall, Liam knew that she'd permanently claimed a large chunk of his heart.

Or maybe she had already claimed *all* of it.

FOURTEEN

MIA

"Are you sure you don't mind that I'm here?" she asked Mandy as they turned the corner that led to the other woman's work area.

"Oh, no," Mandy said. "Most of my work these days comes if someone gets a new injury during a game or practice, or tracking their healing. The post-game stretches and massages and tapings are done by my underlings."

That last was said loudly as they strode through the door into the PT Suite and resulted in a chorus of hissing and boos by the four other people in the room.

"Where are the players?" she asked.

"Showering or still talking to the media," Mandy said. "I think we have approximately two-point-six minutes until the hoard descends." Her volume increased as she addressed the room. "Everyone say, 'Hi, Mia.'"

"Hi, Mia," came the chorus of voices.

Mia waved and said hi back. She'd met Mandy's team two nights before. They seemed nice, albeit busy, and aside from wearing the same black shirt with a Gold logo embroidered above their chest pocket, Mandy's "underlings" were about as different as possible.

Short, tall. Male, female. Rich brown skin, pale white with freckles, tan with hints of olive, porcelain and smooth. The same went for hair—curly and straight, two dark brown, one blonde, one black. It was a cornucopia of diversity in the same space, but the best part about it was the way Mandy's team worked.

An elusive mix of joke and teasing, but with plenty of hard work thrown in.

It had been fun to just sit in the room and listen to the banter two nights before, to experience something different, something she enjoyed, but also something she would never be able to implement with her students.

This was democracy.

She was an autocrat.

But that wasn't exactly true, was it? Her adult classes were different from her children and teen levels. She was the clear leader, obviously, but they did have a lighter feel. Her younger crowd needed discipline, however, and they often needed a rigid structure to focus and stay on task. Banter wouldn't exactly help implement that.

That was just the way it was.

Still, it also didn't mean she couldn't sit back and enjoy being in the mix. "How can I help?" she asked after waving to Aiden, one of the team's massage therapists.

"You can sit your butt down and tell me how Liam went from sad and quiet to grinning like a fool." Mandy pulled open a drawer, started lining up supplies on a tray. "How did you meet? How long have you been together? How—" She stopped, looking up. "I'm doing it again, aren't I?"

Mia was quiet for a moment, blinking from the speed of the conversational shifts and the multitude of questions.

Mandy squeezed her hand. "Sorry," she said. "I forget sometimes that we're used to this."

"Used to what?"

"Everyone being in everyone else's business," Mandy said. "I was joking about getting all the gossip . . . kind of." She lifted her hands, palms up, like she was weighing her options. "We're a family here. The organization tries its best to have that vibe, anyway. And I do think they succeed. We care about each other, not just about hockey and making money, but we also want our team happy."

"And you want to know every detail."

A shrug. "Obviously." She grinned. "We're really nosy, but usually we try to ease people into it."

Mia chuckled. "You'll have to ease me into what exactly?"

"The gossip train"—she lifted a fist like she was blasting a train whistle—"Choo-choo!"

A snort.

"It's true," Mandy said. "It's high speed. Faster than even those trains that run on magnets in Japan."

Mia laughed outright at that. "Well, thanks for letting me know." She sobered, meeting the other woman's eyes, the warmth in those pale brown depths loosening her lips. "In truth, I think I'll need the easing," she said softly, admitting something she wouldn't have dreamed of saying before she'd met Liam. But he'd peeled back the layers, buffed away the sharp edges, made her realize that even though she'd formed her outside in the very image of the person her dad had been—one exactly like him— Mia also still had some of her mom left. It had just been safer to pretend she didn't. It didn't hurt as much, didn't make her as vulnerable.

If she could just be as invulnerable as her dad, then she would be safe.

But . . . that wasn't how she wanted to live forever.

And it had taken Liam for her to realize that.

She inhaled, released it slowly, and forced herself to keep her gaze on Mandy's. "But, another truth, and one that's probably way too much for us barely knowing each other"—apparently getting too attached to people upon first meetings was becoming her superpower, even more so than multitasking—"I-I'm not used to having a family. Or at least, not one like this."

Quiet.

A long, stretching moment of quiet that had pretty brown eyes turning sad.

Mia braced herself, prepped for pity or worse, derision. She'd had too much of both in the last decade.

Instead, Mandy set the roll of tape down and reached over to cover Mia's hand. "Let me preface this by saying, I'm not trying to presume to know what your life is or has been like." She squeezed lightly. "But . . . it's hard for women like us. A sharp learning curve, too much at once until it's almost painful. It's . . . we think that we don't deserve it and—" A deep shuddering breath. "Sometimes I *still* think that. Still struggle. But I also know that at the end of the day, I have my family, the one made by bonds of friendship, of trust, of some really fucking long and hard days." The door opened, players started to come in, and she straightened, letting her hand fall away. "I'll just say this one last thing, Mia. I know how hard it is for us to believe that someone might want us, but, babe, you're valuable, you're important, you *mean* something."

Someone called out Mandy's name before Mia could respond to that, and the trainer bustled off.

It was probably a good thing, as Mia couldn't form words anyway.

You're valuable, you're important, you mean something.

Just words, but also words that cemented Mia's instincts. Mandy was going to be a great mom, or was already, she supposed, but as her daughter got older, she was going to be even better.

You're valuable, you're important, you mean something.

Because her mom had said those same words to her, had driven them home year after year. Even though they'd been buried, tarnished and scratched to faintness by loss, by guilt, they were still there.

And now they were back in the open.

You're valuable, you're important, you mean something.

FIFTEEN

H e walked out of the arena, his fingers laced with Mia's. "Did you drive tonight?" The previous game she'd taken a Lyft, but he didn't want to risk her car sitting in the lot all night.

"No," she said. "I walked."

"Walked?"

Her studio and apartment were near the Castro. The Gold Mine was at the waterfront, almost in the shadow of the Bay Bridge. San Francisco wasn't huge, but that wasn't an easily walkable distance, not by a long shot.

"I was at the Ferry Building," she said. "I—" A shake of her head.

"What?"

Her eyes closed, slowly reopened. "I didn't realize it until during the game, but the memories were chasing me today, pressing down on me from all sides, and I just needed to feel close to her, to go someplace that she loved."

He tugged her to a stop. "Her?" he asked gently.

"My mom." She released a long, slow breath. "I spent a long

time trying to forget everything that happened. But it's like, from the moment I met you"—a shake of her head—"those memories won't stay tucked away."

Her quiet admission was a punch to his gut. He was hurting her? Meeting Mia had helped him start to find his way back to himself, and meanwhile, he was—

"No," she said, the firm word making his eyes snap back to hers. "No, Liam. Not like that."

He turned, cupped her cheek with his free hand. "How can you possibly know what I'm thinking?"

Her hand covered his. "I don't know. It makes no sense. I just —I guess I just feel like I've known you for my whole life. Or maybe that's not right, because I haven't even known *me* for the last ten years." Her eyes filled with tears. "My mom died when I was sixteen. It was my fault, and my dad . . . well, he didn't exactly blame me outright, but I felt that weight all the same."

Fuck.

"Come here, J.B." He tugged her against his chest, began walking them to his car. As much as he was glad she'd opened up to him, as much as he wanted to hear the rest, they were also in a parking lot.

His teammates could come out. Some paparazzi could be lurking.

The Gold had been receiving an inordinate amount of media attention, even before Brit had become the first female to play in the NHL.

Liam didn't want any of that attention shifted to Mia.

So, he bustled her into the back seat of his car and slid in next to her. "I'm so sorry," he whispered, holding her close.

"It was my birthday."

Those words were four slices to his heart.

"Honey," he murmured, stroking a hand up and down her back. "I'm sorry," he said again, not knowing what else to say, knowing that even if he magically found the right sentiment that it wouldn't make her feel better.

There was no healing this kind of pain.

"She loved abalone diving." She leaned back slightly, damp eyes meeting his. "Do you know what that is?"

He shook his head.

"It's like a giant sea snail. You've probably seen the shells around. They're huge. Or at least the ones you're allowed to catch are. A minimum of seven inches wide, nondescript on the outside, but inside they have these beautiful iridescent shells." She swallowed. "People eat the meat, but I haven't been able to stomach it since—"

She broke off, shook her head.

"Well, I can't eat it anymore." Her voice dropped. "But I did then. And so, when my mom asked me what I wanted for my birthday, I asked for abalone soup. I didn't know she was going to go out diving that day. I thought she'd buy some at the Ferry Building. I-I—" A sob. "I wouldn't have asked if I'd known what was going to happen."

"Shh," he said, holding her tighter. "Of course you wouldn't have."

"She went out to her favorite spot. A swell pushed her into a rock. She was a strong swimmer, but I guess . . . she couldn't get out. I don't know if she hit her head or—" Mia dropped her forehead to his collarbone, wrapped her arms tightly around him. "The season is tightly controlled because they're so rare and the population is at risk." A shuddering breath. "You have to free dive, no oxygen tanks, and the underwater cliffs they like to hang out on are full of caves and hideaways that the abalone love but are dangerous for humans."

Bile burned the back of his throat, but Liam forced himself to be still, to hold her, to listen.

"She . . . well, she wasn't there when I came home from school, wasn't back for dinner." Her arms convulsed, voice jagged shards. "I remember being furious she wasn't there. That she'd missed my birthday, hadn't even made the *one* thing I'd asked for." Mia sucked in a breath, released it slowly. "As much as my mom loved having her own business and wanted the karate studio to be successful, she wasn't a martial artist. She couldn't stand the sport, actually. She handled schedules and billing and phone calls . . . and not very well. She was really more at home painting."

He touched her cheek. "What did she paint?" he asked gently.

"Anything." Mia sat up, lips curving. "Used to drive my dad crazy. Every other week there would be a new mural on one of the apartment walls or wet paint in the studio that the kids had to avoid." She chuckled lightly. "He was always happier when she got a commission because the mess would be someone else's problem."

He cupped her jaw, asked softly, "How did your parents end up starting the studio?"

Warmth in her expression. "She wanted my dad to have a place that was his. They'd met in Europe where my dad competed internationally. He even got a gold medal in Judo in 1988. I think because she had her art and was doing well at it, she knew he needed a project, something to keep him busy and engaged when he stopped competing." She brushed her hair out of her face. "They bought the building outright after she sold a commission, and the rest is history. My dad put his focus to good use, made the business successful. My mom kept painting. Eventually, they had me, and we were a happy unit."

Liam cupped the side of her neck, tilted her head until his eyes met hers. "It's not your fault."

"I know." The right words, but her tone told him enough. She didn't really believe that. Not deep down.

"Mia—"

"Did you know I thought she'd gotten distracted by one of the galleries up north?" she said. "I kept thinking she would show up with a pair of earrings made from abalone shell or a necklace or even just a random carving. I just *knew* she'd walk through the door any second, bags stuffed with trinkets from one of the shops along the coast in her hands."

He wiped his thumb beneath each of her eyes, drying her tears. "But she didn't."

"No," Mia murmured. "She didn't."

He waited, just held her close, knowing instinctively there was more she needed to say.

"Then the knock on the door came. It took them a while, you see. Two other divers found her body pinned underwater against some rocks. They tried to help her, but it was too late, and they didn't know who she was or if she had been with anyone." Another tear slipped from the corner of her eye, dripped down her cheek. "Hours later, it became clear there was only one car left in the parking lot, so they got inside it and discovered it was hers —she'd locked her purse inside, along with her ID." A deep breath. "And then they came to the apartment and—" She broke off on a sob.

"Oh, sweetheart."

"It shouldn't hurt this much," she said. "It shouldn't. Not after all these years."

"You're allowed to feel what you feel," he said. "You lost your mom. That hurts. It doesn't just go away because a few years have passed."

"It's been a decade."

He smiled down at her, brushing away her tears. "So good at arguing," he said lightly. "But, J.B., I don't care if it's been a day or a decade, you don't have to justify how you're feeling."

Wide brown eyes. Wide, *soft* brown eyes. "You're such a good guy," she whispered, slipping her hands from around his waist to rest on his shoulders.

He shook his head. "Mia—"

"No," she said. "You're not allowed to argue with me."

"Is that a rule?" he teased.

"It's my rule," she said pertly.

He grinned. "Noted."

"I'm sorry I turned into a blubbering mess," she said.

"If blubbering means you crawl into my lap and put your arms around me, then I'll take it, any day of the week."

She swatted at his chest. "This is you being sensitive?"

"No." He brushed his lips across her forehead. "This is me thanking you for trusting me with that."

Mia stilled, and then her lips curved into a rueful smile. "Good, you see?"

"What I see is a beautiful woman in my arms, who saved my sorry ass from getting flattened by a car," he said. "I see a trusting, lovely woman who's strong and capable and wonderful. I see carrot sticks and kicks. I see someone who can fit right in with the people who are rapidly becoming my new family. And J.B."—he tucked a strand of hair behind her ear—"I see a woman who overcame a tragedy and continues to put one foot in front of the other."

"There's more," she said softly, pain still lacing through the warm brown of her irises. "I haven't even told you everything yet."

He chuckled. "Is this your way of trying to get me to run?"

"I—" She stopped, made a face. Then sighed. "I'm good at pushing people away."

"Well," he said. "I'm good at being stubborn. Plus, I dumped my sad family story on you, remember? If anyone should run, it should be you. You're dating the least successful of all the Williamsons, remember?"

Fingers on his jaw. "You were pretty damned successful tonight."

"You helped with that," he murmured, running his lips along her jaw, nipping at the delicate skin there, needing his mouth on her, but also needing to take away the shadows in her eyes. "Seeing you do your routine—"

"My form," she corrected.

"What?"

"It's called a form. I have to know many of them for my next test and to teach the classes. A routine is for dance. A form is tae kwon do."

"Seeing you do your form," he said, and she smiled at him. "It inspired me. You were smooth and graceful and strong . . . all just practicing on your own. I admired the discipline. And fuck, but you can fly through the air."

A flash of bright white teeth. "So can you. Well, fly across the ice."

"See? That's why we're perfect for each other."

She nibbled at her bottom lip. "What about the other stuff?"

"Do you want to talk about it tonight?" Her face screwed up, and he laughed. "I'm guessing that's a no." She nodded. "Okay, so should we go somewhere for dinner before I drive you home? We've only got one more game at the Gold Mine, and then I'll be on the road for five games. I'd like to spend some time with you."

"I don't think I want dinner."

Liam couldn't ignore the slice of disappointment, but he nodded anyway. "I understand." He started to shift her off him, so he could drive her back to her apartment, but before he could, Mia stretched up and slanted her mouth across his.

When she pulled back, eyes hot, breath coming rapidly, she said, "I don't want dinner. I want you."

Heat arrowing for his cock, need making his hands clench into fists.

"I want to say that can be arranged, but I think the cheese factor for that line is too much, even for me."

She laughed, ran her tongue along his bottom lip. "Say it for me anyway."

"Trouble." He kissed the top of her nose before setting her to the side and reaching for the door handle. "My place or yours, J.B.?" He waggled his brows. "Just saying, I have all the Marvel movies on lock."

She followed him from the car, let him help her into the front seat. "And by *on lock,* do you mean you have the streaming service with all of them?"

A grin. "Maybe." He leaned close, whispered in her ear, "I even pay for it."

Fluttering eyelashes, a mouth quirked into a small smile. "Oh, Liam, you know the words that go straight to my heart."

"I hope so, J.B. I hope so."

He kissed her before she could reply, then ushered her into the passenger's seat before rounding the hood, getting behind the wheel, and taking his woman back to his place.

Sixteen

Mia

"Frankly," she said as Liam let her into a decidedly gorgeous condo, "I'm a little disappointed."

He slanted a glance her way, eyes twinkling.

Clearly, he knew her well enough by now to understand she was teasing. "I expected bachelor pad and I got . . ."

Bachelor pad.

But really nice bachelor pad.

A big couch. A bigger TV mounted on the wall. A spaghetti mess of cords that looked to be a jumble of gaming systems on top of a sleek black entertainment system. No throw pillows or blankets. No curtains.

This was pretty much her place.

Except nicer and more expensive.

But funny if her mom didn't come into the forefront of her mind again, because she had the distinct idea that a bright painting on the wall by the windows would liven up the space, that a couple of blankets and pillows on the couch would make the leather cozier.

Probably, she should start with her place first.

It was austere, could use some soft, and she actually owned it.

Fingers shifting her ponytail aside, lips on her nape. "Why are you smiling?"

Mia turned in the circle of his arms, met stormy gray eyes. Except, they were less storm and more fluffy cloud in the light of his place. "We have the same decorating style."

"Empty Chic?"

She nodded. "I was thinking more like Mid-Century Nothing, but yours works just as well."

A sexy chuckle that arrowed straight between her thighs. "You hungry?"

Mia shook her head.

"Want something to drink?"

Another shake.

"Should we turn on a superhero movie and get lost in Thor's abs?"

Mia burst out laughing.

"God, I love it when you laugh."

She stilled at the reverence in his voice, the soft fingers on her jaw, the warmth in those gray eyes. Never had anyone talked to her like that. Never had they touched her in veneration, looked at her like she might be someone's salvation.

Pain.

Mia had only caused pain.

But not to this man.

To this man, she was different. She was more. She was special. She—

"Liam?" she asked.

"Yeah, J.B.?"

Damn, she needed to find out what the hell that nickname meant. But, more important to this moment, she needed *him*. Clenching her fingers onto the lapels of his suit, a sleek gray number that made her wonder if it was one of those original five suits he'd bought with his first paycheck.

Also, not the point.

"What is it, sweetheart?" he asked, and she realized she'd been quiet too long, focused on the thoughts, her body, her *need* spiraling ever higher.

She traced her fingers over his chest, feeling the row of buttons bump-bump along her palms, soaking in the soft hiss of his breath when her hands slid over the flat, hard planes of his abdomen.

"I don't want to watch a movie."

"Okay," he said. "So, no movie. No drinks. No dinner." He lightly tugged a strand of her hair. "What is it you *do* want?"

What she wanted was *him*. Because she'd moved way past frozen and scared and was firmly in the seize-the-life-in-front-of-her camp. Because Liam was different, was *more* than she'd ever hoped for.

Because he was a good man.

Her man.

A curl of satisfaction slid through her at the last. Yes, *her* man. He was made for her. Hell, they were made for each other with this strong ass connection, the ability to fill in each other's gaps, to complement and make one another better.

And that was just emotionally.

Because physically?

Off the charts.

He was near. She was wet.

Cause. Effect. As simple as that.

"Uh-oh." Liam's voice was hot velvet brushing over her breasts, her stomach, slipping between her thighs and making them clench. "There's that look again." Lips on her jaw, her earlobe. "What went through your mind?"

Seeing as she didn't have anything to lose, Mia told him.

And was rewarded with a kiss so hot that she was surprised her eyebrows weren't singed.

"J.B.?" he asked, one hand clamped to her hip, the other woven into her hair.

"Hmm?" She didn't even care about the nickname, not when

his mouth was so close to hers, not when she was plastered against him, not when need was a hot brand sliding over her skin.

"Are you sure you're wet?"

His hand slipped in, fingertips just beneath the waistband of her jeans.

Her breath caught, stymieing any sort of quippy answer she might have come up with.

Rough callouses on smooth skin. His fingers undoing the button of her jeans, sliding the tag of her zipper down.

"Maybe I should check," he murmured, lips resting against hers, words vibrating against her mouth . . . and all the while those fingers slid lower, crept nearer. His hand was inside her jeans, beneath the cotton of her underwear. So close. So far. And fuck, but she wanted this man.

"Enough," she growled, clamping her arms around Liam's shoulders, leaping into his arms, and slanting her mouth on his. "Show me to your bedroom," she snapped, glaring into his mischievous gray eyes. "Otherwise, I'm taking you to the ground here and now."

A smirk.

A twitch of a finger just above her clit.

She wasn't kidding. She shifted her body weight, rotated her arms and legs in a quick flick of a movement.

And then he was on the ground.

Beneath her.

"Mmm," he murmured, seemingly not bothered by the move.

She *had* taken him down slowly, cushioning him against the brunt of the impact. Still, if the hands gripping her hips, the hard-ass cock between pressing against her, hitting that perfect spot as she straddled him was any indication, he didn't mind being beneath her.

"Why do I suddenly feel the need to be wearing cowboy boots?" she asked, resting more of her weight against him.

He thrust up, pressing the seam of her jeans against her clit. "*Just* cowboy boots?"

"Well, obviously," she said, though her pert reply was lost when she moaned as he thrust against her again. It was glorious and not enough, and suddenly she was cursing all of the layers between them. "Why do you still have your pants on?" she grumbled.

"You're the one who got us into this predicament," he pointed out.

She made a face. "I'll take this moment to reiterate that I wanted you to show me to your bedroom."

"It's more Mid-Century Empty," he said, hissing out a breath when she reached down and began undoing the button on his slacks.

"I thought it was Mid-Century Nothing," she asked, mouth watering.

She'd tugged down the zipper on his pants, separated the fabric, revealing his black boxer briefs. Black cotton that was currently stretched very tightly over his cock. A very large, very hard, very—

"Are you going to keep staring at it?" he asked hoarsely.

"Yes," she murmured, thinking the sight of him mostly dressed, sprawled out beneath her, the tight cotton emphasizing more than it hid was the most intoxicating thing she'd ever laid eyes on. In fact, the longer she stared down at him, the bigger and harder he grew, until a hint of the tip of his cock had appeared, slipping out from beneath the waistband of his underwear. She traced a finger over the silken steel. "It's like a magic trick. Out of my hat I pull a—*ack!*"

Mia was strong.

Mia was used to sparring, to grappling with men bigger and larger than her.

But Liam was an athlete.

He was just as strong. He was just as fast.

And she found *she* didn't mind being the one sprawled out beneath him.

Especially when her shoes were yanked off her feet, landing

with twin thumps somewhere in the direction of the door. Especially when her jeans followed suit, when her arms were coaxed up, her sweater and T-shirt tugged over her head in one quick move.

She pushed at his jacket and he obliged her, shoving it down his arms, launching it to the side at the same time as she began working at the buttons of his shirt, fumbling to slip the circles of plastic through the holes because his fingers had moved down—

"Oh fuck!" she cried out, bucking against him when his palm ground against her clit, making stars flash behind her eyes, pleasure shoot through her limbs.

Found it on the first try. No roadmap, GPS, or headlamp required.

God, this man was perfect for her in so many ways.

And perhaps the best one was that he didn't need a floodlight and those airport signaling thingies to find her clit.

She grinned at the thought, but then just as quickly the thought disappeared . . . because her panties were gone, tossed in the direction of her jeans, and leaving her bottomless.

One leg over his shoulder.

The other.

And then his mouth was on her.

She cried out, throwing her head back as sparks flowed through her body, desire inundating every cell, every nerve. There was no fumbling about, no missing the key bits, no need for her to direct or multitask—trying to position him correctly while also trying to get there.

When he discovered what she liked, he did it again.

When she moaned, he repeated the action.

When she squirmed, hips seeking purchase, he gave her more pressure.

When she felt empty, her pussy convulsing with a growing ache, he filled her, one finger slipping inside, curling forward, finding a spot that made her brain shut down and her body just feel.

And *how* it felt.

So much heat threatening to reduce her to ashes.

So much desire ramping higher and higher until her muscles trembled from the strain, until she was perched on that precipice and. So. Fucking. Close.

Which was when he pulled out the big guns, doing something with his tongue that should have been illegal. She could have sworn she'd gone blind for a moment or at the very least, blacked out as pleasure swelled up, bursting over her in a tidal wave of sensation, filling every part of her body with complete and utter bliss.

It could have been seconds or minutes or hours as wave after wave after wave spread through her, but when she finally came to, Liam was next to her. He had three buttons undone but was otherwise dressed.

"I'm bottomless and you're clothed," she muttered. "Not fair."

His fingers—still between her thighs—twitched, sending little flurries of pleasure throughout her. "I like you bottomless."

Mia smiled, unable to stop herself. "Well, I *like* you, Liam. Too damned much considering we've known each other for *maybe* two weeks, if we're counting this being the second week."

"I stopped counting when I saw you moving on the other side of the glass."

Her lungs froze.

"I definitely stopped counting when you kissed me at the bottom of that slide, where you twisted my arm and made me break all the rules—"

"Hey!"

His fingers twitched again, cutting off her protest, lips parting on a moan, and he took full advantage, dropping his mouth to hers and kissing her until she'd forgotten all of what she'd planned to say.

Lips on her chin, her throat, her collarbone, the tops of her breasts.

"I stopped thinking," he said, against her skin. "Because I wanted to feel."

Feel.

Well, his mouth felt good. His fingers, his hands, his body all felt incredible. His soft words, his gentle teasing . . . they made her feel complete.

And she had the fleeting thought, right before his mouth slid up from her breasts to slant across her mouth, that perhaps she was more like her dad than she'd given herself credit for. Maybe it was less mask, less trying to be the person he'd wanted her to be. Maybe she was just like him in the sense that there was only one being on the planet, in the universe that could fit perfectly into her heart.

If that person was gone, she would turn into a shell. Like her dad had.

If that person left, *she* wouldn't have anything left. Just like her dad, who had simply faded away, year after year getting smaller, disappearing into himself, forgetting about everything except for the hurt of the present, his memories of a past that had been wonderful, and the bleakness of a future that would never be complete.

A bolt of panic shot through her.

She could see that path so clearly, knew in her heart of hearts that was why she'd avoided any connections.

He'd pretended to be hard and unaffected, too.

But he hadn't been.

He'd been soft underneath.

And when he'd been hurt, that soft had never recovered.

So, he'd made Mia hard. Given her armor, ways to protect herself.

Perhaps it was less wanting more than she should have, less disappointment, less hating her for being a selfish sixteen-year-old, who'd unintentionally been responsible for a tragedy.

Perhaps, by taking everything away, he'd been trying to protect her.

Her breath caught. Her lungs froze.

She nearly twisted out of Liam's hold.

But by then he was already scooping her up into his arms, by then he was already cradling her close, by then she was surrendering to the man who'd taken everything in her life and shaken it all to the core.

All of those parts rattled around, pieces falling this way and that, uncertain of what would land and what would float away. Heads up or down, breaking into pieces, colliding with a solid *thunk*. Mia couldn't be sure of how everything would turn out, because Liam was holding her.

Because then Liam was kissing her.

And she tucked everything down to deal with in the future. This was a time to feel, to stop her multitasking superpowers, to be in the moment and focus on the man she *liked*, the man she was falling for, the man she might already be half in love with but was too damned scared to admit it all the same.

Fingers threaded into her hair, tilted her head back, lips gentle and coaxing.

The thoughts fell away.

The sensations rose up.

She turned herself over to the moment.

SEVENTEEN

LIAM

He had a beautiful woman in his arms, and she'd all but demanded he take her to his bedroom.

Yeah, his life wasn't turning out to be *too* bad.

Especially when she kissed him until his legs went shaky in a way that was definitely not post-game fatigue but was certainly all about the power of Mia.

After striding across the room, he dropped her to the mattress, fingers yanking at the buttons of his shirt until he somehow managed to undo them. He fought with the cuffs for several long moments before Mia helped, unbuttoning them and pushing the cotton off his arms.

It landed on the carpet in a near soundless murmur.

But *she* wasn't soundless. "Off," she demanded, shoving the waistband of his slacks down, making him scramble for a few seconds to kick off his shoes before he tripped over the material—now at his thighs—and landed on his ass again.

At least this time it was on the mattress.

One shoe then the other slipped free. His pants hit the floor a heartbeat later.

And then he had the glorious opportunity to watch Mia reach behind her and unhook her bra.

He didn't have a clue where that scrap of material landed because . . . breasts.

Glorious, luscious breasts with dusky nipples that his mouth actually ached to taste.

So he did, bending to take one hard peak in his mouth and suckle deep, to taste the sweetness of her skin, the slight tang of salt. Ambrosia, and he wanted so much more. He wanted to be a glutton, to inhale every bite, to lick and nip and taste . . . and he didn't know where to start.

Mia didn't have that problem.

She took his hand, leaned back onto the mattress, and tugged him on top of her. "Kiss me, Liam."

An easy order to follow, he let his lips fall to hers, allowed himself the opportunity to learn her skin, her curves. He'd had her come on his tongue and yet there were so many soft spots he didn't know. Places that made her shiver, some that made her moan. He wanted to know every single secret that was hidden within her body.

Sliding his hand up her side, noting the slight squirm of a ticklish spot at her ribs, he continued moving until he was cupping her breast, until the hard bud of her nipple was against his palm. She moaned, head thrown back, and he took the opportunity to kiss his way down to her glorious fucking breasts, to taste her again, only this time to give the luscious curves the time they deserved.

"Liam!"

Fuck, but he loved the way she cried out his name.

He sucked a nipple deeply into his mouth, pinched her other one between thumb and forefinger, needing to taste her, loving the way she reacted to his touch, his lips, his tongue.

And then she slid her hand into his underwear, wrapping her fingers around his cock and squeezing hard enough that his eyes rolled back.

Because he fucking loved the way her touch made him feel.

Alive, burning with need, one firm stroke away from shattering into pieces.

Heat coiled at the base of his spine, red sparks entered the edges of his vision, and Liam knew he was in trouble.

Brushing those dangerous fingers aside was harder than he expected.

Well, probably because he wasn't trying *that* hard to get her hand off his cock, not when she was stroking him exactly as he liked—firm, a little rough, and fast—

He groaned, finally managed to pull her off.

Because as good as it felt to have her hands on him, she had also been stroking fast enough that if she kept going, this would all be over way sooner than he wanted. Than *she* wanted.

"Liam," she groaned, reaching for him again.

He blocked her, grinned down at her, amused despite the haze of desire clouding his vision. "You're kind of feisty, J.B.," he said, nuzzling her neck, knowing that she could easily get free from his grip if she wanted. Which made her staying there, fingers sliding into his hair and tugging back his head to mock-glare up at him, though her eyes were dancing with amusement, mean so much more.

"You'll tell me the meaning of that nickname."

A nip to the inside of her forearm. "Not today."

Fingers tightening for a brief second before softening, before one leg came up to wrap around his hip. "When?"

He grinned. "With the right motivation."

"Is you about to be inside me *not* proper motivation?"

"It's *a* motivation." He traced his fingers along the inside of her thigh, slid higher. "But I'd rather be talking less and—"

She flipped them.

One second, he was touching the damp heat of her pussy, and the next he was flat on his back. Her hands came to his chest, her eyes narrowed. "Condom."

Fuck, but she was the sexiest woman he'd ever met.

Shifting, he reached into the nightstand, pulled one out, but before he could tear it open, she snagged it from him, ripped off the corner with her teeth, and then proceeded to tease him to insanity as she rolled it, millimeter by infinitesimal millimeter down his cock.

Sweat dripped down his back. His fingers shook with the need to tug her over him, to pull her down and slide inside.

He strived for patience, for finesse, for—

Mia hopped off his thighs, smug smile on her lips as she pulled down his boxer briefs. One firm kick and they were gone, and he expected her to get back on top of him, to take him deep while he played with her breasts . . . or maybe that was just one of a litany of fantasies.

Instead, she surprised him.

He should be used to that, her putting him on the back foot by now, but he was still frozen for a moment, shocked into stillness for several heartbeats when she lay back on the mattress, head on the pillow next to him, when the soft words laced with desire reach his ears.

"Come inside me," she said and spread her legs.

If the sentiment hadn't done it, seeing her thighs inch apart, giving a teasing glimpse of a wet pussy he could still taste on his tongue would have shattered the final vestiges of his control.

He was on top of her before he registered moving, and the feel of her naked body against his had his brain shorting out, his mind flickering to a halt.

Feel.

It was finally time to just feel.

His palm tracing her side, his mouth on her breasts, his fingers dipping down between her thighs, circling her clit, loving the way she arched up on a moan, unable to resist her when she tugged him over her, demanding, "Now!"

It was in his nature to slow down to try and make this perfect, but he'd learned over the last few weeks.

Learned that sometimes he didn't have to worry about every

detail, sometimes he could use his instincts, let sensation take over, and just be in this moment with Mia.

He hitched her leg over his waist, positioned himself at her opening—

She wrapped her other leg around him and pulled him down.

They both moaned as he pushed inside, and he was overwhelmed by the sensations—she was tight and hot, her body flush against his, her arms and legs wrapped snuggly around him, but it was more than just pleasure and nerve endings because he also felt full, complete in a way he'd never experienced.

Not just like. Love.

Not just sex. More.

Not just this moment. Forever.

Then she shifted, pussy clenching around him, and he had to match the movements. He had to *move*. In and out. Slow and steady. Speeding up, pressing harder, thrusting deeper until he didn't know where he ended and she began.

"More," she gasped, hands in his hair, legs wrapped tight. "More, Liam."

He gave her more. He gave her *everything*.

And then he continued giving as he moved, as he stroked and caressed, as he bent and took her lips in a kiss that transmuted every ounce of what he was feeling into touch, into taste, into perfection.

Her head fell back, breathing rapid, moans increasing in volume, but she wasn't quite there. He thrust hard, found the angle that made her muscles clench around him, and slid a hand to press his thumb against her clit. She hissed out a breath, but he didn't stop, didn't wait, just bent to suck a nipple deep and kept moving.

His abs burned like a motherfucker. Sweat dripped down his forehead, getting in his eyes and stinging like hell.

But nothing was more important than this woman in this moment.

Nothing.

She cried out, going stiff for several heartbeats before melting beneath him, falling over the edge, pleasure making her limbs heavy. He didn't stop moving. He couldn't have, not when his own edge was there, so close his fingertips were already grazing the cliffside.

"Come inside me, baby," she murmured again, legs squeezing him tight, pussy still convulsing around him.

The words. The way she held him.

The glazed look of pleasure in her eyes.

That was all he needed.

He was already gone.

Eighteen

Mia

He'd collapsed on top of her.

He was sweaty. And heavy.

But she didn't ask him to move.

Because this was Liam. Because this was the man she was falling for, the man who'd rocked her world and sent her shattering before carefully catching all the pieces and gluing her back together.

And also . . . because he was sexy and had just given her two of the best orgasms of her life.

It wasn't exactly a trial to hold him close as he lay on top of her, his cock still hard inside her, his body pressed against hers.

He kissed her neck, shifted to the side, tugging her against his chest. "You okay?"

"That's a stupid question," she said.

A chuckle that ruffled her hair. "It may be," he said, tone light, "but, are you okay?" It was the edge of concern in his voice that made her look at him, to study those gray eyes, now clouded with apprehension.

Her heart rolled over in her chest.

This man. This *good* man.

"Because of the fan-fucking-tastic sex?" she asked, rubbing her nose along his collarbone. He was a little sweaty still, so it should have been gross, but there was something about this man's scent. It was her catnip and she wanted to roll around in him. "Or because of my blubbering earlier?"

Fingers under her chin, coaxing it up, encouraging her eyes to meet his. "J.B."

Just J.B.

That was it.

A quiet admonishment.

"I'm fine," she told him.

"Mia—"

"No," she said, wrapping her hand around his wrist, squeezing lightly. "I'm serious. It's like . . . everything hurt so much more when it was all tangled up inside me. But being able to talk about it, to have someone listen without judgment makes me feel lighter." She cupped the side of his neck, brushed her lips over his. "*You* make me feel lighter."

He ran his knuckles along her cheek. "Have you not talked to anyone about it before?"

Mia remembered what it had been like after going back to school, how she'd felt so removed from her classmates, how she couldn't relate to her friends. They'd tried to reach out, but unless they'd gone through it, what sixteen-year-old kid really understood losing a parent?

"It wasn't like people shut me out, but I also think it was hard for them to relate, to find the right thing to say." She sighed. "And then there was everything that happened with my dad."

He paused. "Is this the more?"

She nodded. "And I'll admit, I'm still struggling to understand, to know what I'm feeling now, what his motivations were, because for so long I thought he blamed me for what happened, and now . . ."

"Now what?" he asked when she ran out of steam. He rolled

onto his back, gathered her close so she was sprawled on top of him.

"Now, I wonder if he was trying to protect me." She crossed her arms on his chest and rested her chin on them. "Or, I don't know. Maybe not. Maybe it's like I thought as a teenager—that he blamed me, wanted to teach me to not ask for more than I should." She sighed. "Or . . . maybe it's what I'd come to think over the last few years. He was hurting so much that he needed to erase everything about my mom. Because if he didn't see her day after day, then it was easier to go on."

Liam rested his hand on the small of her back. "Erase, how?"

"A few days after her funeral, I came home from school, and he'd packed it all up—her paintings, her jewelry, her clothes. Knickknacks she'd picked up on her travels. He'd even painted over the half-finished mural on the walls of my bedroom, had gotten rid of the pillows on the couch."

"Shit," he breathed. "J.B.—"

"I thought he was punishing me." She sighed. "And maybe he was. But also . . . maybe it wasn't so clear cut because I think of what I feel for you, after knowing you for so short a time, and I know I would be devastated if you were just . . . gone."

He got a sick look on his face, one that made her insides twist themselves into knots.

"What is it?" she asked.

"One day, I *might* be gone," he said quietly. "If I get traded—"

She relaxed, pushed up enough to touch his cheek. "That's different."

"I know," he said. "I'm sorry. I wasn't trying to make this about me. I just—" A shake of his head. "I don't want to hurt you, sweetheart."

Mia smiled at him. "What happened to J.B.?"

A solemn look. "I didn't think this was a time for teasing."

"Don't," she said. Her tone was intense, too intense, she knew it was. Except . . . she needed him to understand this. To not change for her.

He frowned. "Don't what?"

She released a shaking breath. "Don't stop teasing me. Don't stop being you. Don't stop pushing me to break all of my rules." Her eyes burned, but she'd cried enough for the night, so she blinked the tears back. "I felt so guilty for so long that I didn't push back. I just kept pulling into myself. When he got rid of my mom's stuff, I didn't argue. I thought I deserved it." His curse had her sinking back into his arms, hugging him tight. "It's okay. I understand now . . . or, at least, I think I do."

"That wasn't right, J.B."

"I know." She sighed. "He shouldn't have done that. Maybe I'll never know if he did that—the erasing of my mom—to protect himself or to protect me, but I don't believe any longer that he was trying to punish me."

"I'm glad." His kiss over her forehead was a whisper of contact.

"I mean, he's gone now, he had a heart attack five years ago, so I won't ever have the answer, but I do think . . . he tried to make my world smaller so that I would be safe." Liam was quiet as she spoke, his fingers tracing gentle patterns on her skin, but she could tell he had questions, thoughts, even though he was trying to let her work it in her own brain and out loud. "What are you thinking?"

"That I'm glad he's gone."

She recoiled at the venom in his words, his eyes that were filled with frost. "I know that's inappropriate, that I shouldn't say that about your dad, but what the fuck, J.B.? When you have a kid, it stops being about you. Your job is to put them first, to make their life better. To raise them to be a healthy adult." His palm slid up her back, rested on the side of her neck, keeping her close as his voice softened. "I'm sorry, but you're so fucking wonderful. It kills me to think of you burying yourself when you didn't have to."

"You're right," she said. "He didn't handle it correctly. He should have told me he didn't blame me, helped me be the person he and my mom were raising me to be before she died." A sigh. "But he didn't. And because of that guilt, because I wanted to make him proud, to not disappoint him further, I got smaller."

His expression was thunderous, but his hold gentle.

"Shh," she said, smoothing her fingers over the stark lines near his mouth, above and between his brows, radiating out from his eyes. "I decided I'm not doing that anymore."

Gentle crept in, pushed out storm clouds. "Just like that?"

She nodded. "Just like that." Shifting, she settled her forehead against his. "So, can you keep pushing and teasing and breaking the rules? I'm going to do my best to find that sixteen-year-old girl again, but it's easy to fall back into old patterns."

"Can you shoot for eighteen rather than sixteen?" he asked, lips twitching. "Gotta keep things legal."

Her heart swelled. This man.

"I'm guessing that's a yes for the teasing?" she asked lightly. "But not the rule-breaking?"

A dark look, though his mouth was curved into a gentle smile. "There are some rules that can't be broken."

"True."

"What's that face?" His fingers traced the lines of her eyebrows, the angle of her jaw.

"That's everything," she whispered. "All of the sad. All of the heavy secrets."

Traces of a storm on the edges of his irises. "And you think what, that I'm going to leave now?"

"It's a lot for two weeks of acquaintance."

He sighed, tugged her down so that she was sprawled across his chest. "I was a lot after a few *hours* of acquaintance," he said. "Just in case you've forgotten my mini-meltdown."

"There were no tears, so it doesn't count."

Laughter that filled her with warmth. "Good to know, J.B."

He hugged her tight, stifled a yawn. "I'll summon some up next time."

She rested her palm on his chest, felt his heart beating slow and steady beneath her hand. "You've impressed me with your pillow talk, Stormy, but you played a tough game. You need your rest."

"Stormy?"

Her cheeks went a little warm. "I'm trying out nicknames, Sweet Cheeks, since you have yours for me."

"I veto both of those names."

"Good thing you don't get to decide."

Fingers brushing through her hair. "What does Stormy mean?"

She tsked. "Nice try. But I'll only do a tit for tat exchange."

"I—" His yawn wasn't stifled this time. "I get it," he said. "My eyes."

Damn. Back to the drawing board because she couldn't honestly see herself using Sweet Cheeks on a daily basis.

He bent, nearly dislodging her from his chest. "Yup," he said, seeing her face. "I knew you'd be pouting." His lips brushed hers. "Still beautiful, even though I won't dish on the nickname meaning."

Warmth in her belly, her heart, her soul.

"Now," he said before she could respond to that, "not to be a wimp, but you tired me out."

"Not the game?" she teased.

Another yawn, a gentle caress brushing her hair off her face. "Not the game," he murmured, voice drifting off, sleep creeping up. "Need anything before I pass out?"

Mia snuggled closer, smile on her lips. "Nope. I just need you."

A kiss to the top of her head, arms wrapping tighter.

Then they fell into sleep.

———

"I thought—" Liam stopped, winced. "Never mind."

She reached across the table. "What were you going to ask?"

"It's—" A shake of his head.

"Solid Gold," she warned. His brows drew down, and damn, she'd known that nickname wouldn't work, even before she'd said it out loud. "No fair." It was a mutter. "You came up with J.B. and all I've got is weirdness."

He lifted her fingers to his mouth. "I like your weirdness."

Heat trailing up her arm, down her spine.

He'd woken her in the most delicious way that morning, kissing his way across her stomach.

When she'd protested that they hadn't showered the night before, he'd given her a slice of dirty that had sent her flying.

"I'm starting my Cheat Day off with my favorite meal," he'd said then had proceeded to move lower, to give her an orgasm with his mouth even before the last bit of sleep had left her mind.

And yet even though they were now in public, at a restaurant eating breakfast . . . she wanted him again.

"Nice try avoiding my questions," she grumbled, tucking that desire away. She'd jump him later. "But what were you going to ask a minute ago?"

"Well, when we grabbed breakfast last week, you said you'd never eaten there or had a lot of junk food." He shrugged. "I guess the way I was imagining your mom, I'd think there would be lots of sugar and treats."

Mia laughed. "I could see how you'd think that. But my mom was a total hippie. No sugar. No processed foods. No salt. We only ate protein we'd caught ourselves, which meant we were mostly vegetarian with the exception of any fish or abalone she brought home when she went to the coast a few times a year, and bacon. My mom always said she could give up a lot of things, but she couldn't give up bacon." She smiled. "I still get my bacon and eggs from the same farmer's market a few blocks from my apartment. Cage-free. No antibiotics. Fresh. Local."

He grinned. "Hippie."

"Exactly."

"Is this where I shouldn't tell you that with three boys at home and competing hockey schedules, we subsisted mostly on processed foods?"

She gave a mock-sigh. "Yup. Total deal-breaker, that one."

Liam chuckled. "Good," he said, scooping up a bite of chocolate chip pancakes that he'd liberally doused with syrup, even though they had been delivered to the table already coated with powdered sugar. "I won't tell you then." He shoved the bite into his mouth.

"How do you not have diabetes?"

A shrug. "Every man has his vices."

She primly took a bite of her egg white omelet. Then she pointed. "Hey, is that Mandy?"

Liam glanced over his shoulder. "Where?"

Mia switched the plates, sliding her omelet toward him while stealing his pancakes. She might not have much of a sweet tooth, but even she had to admit they looked delicious.

He turned back. "I don't see her. Are you sure you saw her?"

A shrug. "I guess I'm seeing things."

Liam dipped his fork down, scooped up a bite without glancing at his plate. Instead, his eyes were on hers. "What time do you have to be back?"

"My Mom and Ninja class is at 11:30 am, though I need to do a fair amount of setup for it."

"I can help."

Her heart bubbled with joy even though she asked, "Are you sure you want to spend your day off scrubbing mats and herding kids?"

"I'm sure I want to spend my day off with you, whatever form that takes."

Aw. Her heart skipped a beat. "Then mats it is." He had a bite of egg white hanging from his fork, suspended a few inches off his plate, and Mia began to feel a little guilty for her prank. The man was spending his day off with her, had offered to clean mats and chase toddlers, and meanwhile, she was corrupting one of his Cheat Days, of which he only got a max of one per week. "Li—"

"Is it because Blane is coming?"

"Yes," she said. "Li—"

"You should really consider renaming it Parent and Ninja or something, especially if you want to entice the rest of the hockey guys to come and take the class," he said. "And with the rate the team is going, there'll be a whole tiny Gold army invading." The fork drifted closer. She opened her mouth, but Liam kept talking. "Blue even pulled me aside yesterday before the game. His son is a few months younger than Mandy and Blane's daughter, so he wanted to join in the class. I hope it's okay that I gave him your number."

"Yes, of course. I'm sure that's fine, but—"

The fork went into his mouth.

For all of a second, then it was back out, Liam's face one of disgust as he chewed. She had to give him credit for not spitting out the bite. She might have, had she been expecting fluffy pancakes and getting a semi-chewy omelet.

This breakfast place wasn't as good as the one around the corner from her house.

His eyes flicked down at the plate in front of him then over to the plate in front of her, and figuring she was already in for a penny, she scooped up a bite and plunked it into her mouth.

Then winced.

Because it was a straight shock of sugar.

That was *it*. Sugar.

Ha.

Mia affected her best innocent expression. "Is there a problem?" she asked, scooping up another bite but not quite able to shove it into her mouth.

"Nope."

He grinned, nodded at her plate. "You going to eat that, J.B.?"

"Are *you* going to eat *that*, Sugar?" She nodded at his plate.

"Sugar?" One brow came up.

She lifted both of hers. "J.B.?"

His eyes warmed. "God, I love you."

Her fork hit the table, her jaw nearly followed suit.

Meanwhile, Liam set his utensil calmly on his plate then stretched across the worn Formica top and kissed her. "Ignore me if it freaks you out," he murmured before sitting back. "I know it's crazy and too soon. But . . ."

"But what?" she breathed.

"But . . . it's true." Clear gray eyes on hers. "It's insane. It's too much. It's probably going to make you run out of this restaurant and—"

No, it wasn't.

Because, yes it *was* too soon, too fast, too much.

But . . . she felt the same way.

And even though it was a little terrifying—feeling this way for someone when she had been closed down for so long—she loved (yes, *loved!*) Liam too much to leave him hanging in this.

She stood up, ignoring the flash of pain that crossed his face when her feet hit the floor, then rounded the table and dropped into the booth next to him.

Her words were for his ears only.

Leaning close, she whispered, "I love you, too."

His shoulders stiffened. *His* jaw dropped open, and he turned to face her, slowly, incrementally, as though he were afraid he was just hearing things and that she'd poof away if he moved too fast.

"What did you say?"

She picked up the fork, slid her plate closer to her. "You heard me, Sugar."

Fingers on her throat, brushing lightly along the place her pulse was pounding even despite the cavalier words. "I did hear you," he murmured. A kiss to her jaw before his voice rose, lifting to normal volume. "I also do not support that nickname."

"What's J.B. mean?"

A flash of stubborn, bright as lightning in those pretty gray eyes.

"Sugar's here to stay," she said, scooping up a bite of omelet. "Unless you give up the goods."

"That's blackmail."

A shrug. "That's life with a stubborn as shit black belt."

He grinned. "Guess I'd better get used to it."

She smiled back. "Guess you'd better."

"Good thing I'm good at cleaning mats," he teased.

She laughed, light and fluffy, fully in the moment, totally enamored with this man. "Good thing."

Sitting next to the man who'd taken over her heart, who'd made her feel and hope and grow—all in a couple of weeks—Mia knew she would never go back to being the woman she'd been before.

And that was okay with her.

In fact, it was pretty damned perfect.

Nineteen

Liam

His phone buzzed when he was at the bottom of a dog pile of toddlers, so it took Liam a moment to extract himself and pull his phone from his pocket.

His agent was calling.

His agent *never* called.

Unless it was bad news.

Dread curled like a lead ball in his stomach, but he knew he wouldn't be traded at this point in the year. It was past the trade deadline. He was here for the remainder of the season. And his contract was only one-way—which meant that if the team sent him down to the minors, he'd still be paid his contract rate. That had been enough of a motivation for his former teams to keep him in the league, even if he'd been scratched from the actual game roster too many times to count.

As he was staring at the screen, the call cut off.

"Shit," he muttered under his breath, still untangling himself from the toddlers and hoping that at several feet above them, they hadn't heard the curse. He didn't need to add corrupting young children to his list of skills.

So maybe he wouldn't be traded, but the call couldn't be good news. He'd been hoping to have enough time in San Francisco, to keep making a dent in the past fuck ups, to put the puck in the net, to get on the scoresheet with assists, to work his ass off in the defensive end.

He'd wanted more time to make himself valuable.

He wanted to stay.

Because of Mia, but also because of Brit, Blane, Coop, Blue. Because of Mandy and Calle and even the two Rebeccas, despite them nagging him about social media presence and how much animal protein he consumed—each nag only important to one of the Rebeccas, of course. Because the Gold were the Holy Grail. They were the team he'd hoped but never expected to find.

They . . . well, he'd been able to be himself.

And Liam hadn't had that since he was a teenager.

That thought had him looking up, his heart constricting because Mia had experienced the same thing, only hers was exponentially more difficult to reconcile. She'd been through so damned much and—

A sharp whistle drew the rug rats' attention, and the trio still clinging to his shins released, hurrying to the front of the room to get what appeared to be a stamp.

All except for a little boy with pale blue eyes.

"Up!" he said, lifting his arms.

Despite the ice in his heart, the resultant nerves from the missed call, the lingering pain in knowing what he would be losing because this was probably a courtesy call letting him know that the end was nigh, the request still made Liam smile. In fact, he'd gotten quite used to this particular request over the last few hours. So much so that he knew he would be skipping arms and shoulders during his gym time the next day.

"Up!" the little boy demanded.

"Oh no," his mom, a pretty brunette with an intoxicating laugh, said. "Mr. Liam is all done today."

His—the toddler, not Liam's—lip slid out into a pout, eyes filling with tears.

This was also a look that Liam had gotten familiar with.

He knelt. "We're all done for today, bud." The little boy's face screwed up. "Race you to the stamps!" Liam took off, and as he'd hoped, the little boy trailed him, giggling now as he ran by.

"Thanks," the mom said, shaking her head.

"No worries. I'm one of three," he told her. "My mom always said we gave her three gray hairs hourly."

The woman laughed. "I could see that. He's only a three-nager and he's already doing that." She tugged at her ponytail, grays not visible to Liam's gaze, not that he was going to comment on that either way. He did have *some* common sense. "Sometimes I wish I was his age," she said, moving after him as he closed in on Mia and the stamp pad, "then I would be able to stick out my lip and get my way."

"That doesn't work?" he teased.

She giggled. "If it did, I'd have been able to convince my husband to get that Tory Birch diaper bag."

Liam grinned. "Might be worth a second try."

Another giggle as she jogged to the front, scooping up the squirming toddler and tucking him under one arm. "Come on, Trouble."

Mia came over to him. "Everything okay?"

For a second, he thought she might have been jealous of the conversation and started to reassure her that it had just been harmless banter. Then he realized she wasn't looking at the mom at all. Her eyes were on his cell.

Which buzzed, right on cue with a text from his agent.

Call me.

And the lighthearted banter that had managed to distract him was gone.

"Who is that?"

"My agent."

She stilled, and he knew she understood with just those two words. "Will they trade you?"

He shook his head. "No. My contract is up and it's beyond the deadline, but they can say they don't want me back."

"But wouldn't they wait until later in the season?" Her brows drew together. "I mean, I'm not an expert, but the playoffs are coming up. This might be a good thing. Wouldn't they—"

A tug on her leg had her glancing down. "Bye, Ms. Mia."

She patted the little girl's head. "Bye, Ms. Lily."

Lily smiled and ran back to her mom, who waved and headed for the door. Liam glanced around, saw that most of the other parents were occupied, including Blane, who'd brought Madeline in for her class. But there were a few other moms hovering nearby, clearly wanting to talk to Mia.

He touched her cheek. "Deal with what you need to," he murmured. "I'll just step outside and return the call."

"I'm sorry—" she began.

"Don't you dare apologize," he told her firmly. "This is your job, and it's important to you, to *them*." He let his hand drop, knuckles skating down her throat, her arm. "It's important to me."

"I love you," she whispered.

The dread eased. Because, ultimately, hockey wasn't the most important thing in his life any longer. He had Mia. He had himself. He had his family, who loved him even though they meddled. He had friends, new from the team, old built over the years. He would be okay, no matter what. "I love you, too, J.B."

"Silly man." A rueful smile, a shake of her head, and he knew it was the nickname that had garnered the reaction. "Use my office."

He nodded, crossed over to it, and closed the door behind him.

Then he sucked in a breath.

This didn't matter. It didn't matter.

It *did* matter, regardless of how much he wanted to shove the nerves and fear down, to pretend he was cool either way. He wanted to keep playing, and he really wanted to do it with the Gold.

He tapped his screen, dialed his agent.

Ring-ring.

Ring-ring.

Ring—

"Liam."

"Hey, Ron," he said. "How's it going?"

"Fine. Look," Ron said in his typical no-nonsense-don't-have-time-for-small-talk way. It had always been that way, but it had gotten more prevalent over the years. Liam was supposed to have been big time, and he hadn't brought the same capital and clout as his father and brothers.

Hello, Dread. Thanks for joining him again.

"The Gold want to have a sit-down with you. I'm in New York, negotiating some sticky terms, so I can't fly out there. Do you want to meet with them, see what they have to say? Then you and I can discuss?" The statements were clipped out, incongruous with his smooth Texan drawl. "Liam?"

He blinked, forced himself to focus. "That's fine. When do they want to sit down?"

"This afternoon or tomorrow."

Get it over with? Or sit on it, ruminating until the next day? It wasn't even a decision. He wanted to know his fate, and the sooner, the better. He'd deal. He'd make the best of it.

"This afternoon," he told Ron.

"Great. I'll text you a time." The sound of papers rustling interspersed with his agent's words, but the noise wasn't loud enough to drown out the reality of them. Or maybe, it was just that Liam had known this was coming. "You need to prepare for the reality that they will likely not be offering you a good deal or any contract at all," Ron said. "Your stats have improved since you joined the team, but—"

"They're not there yet."

"Right."

"Also, do not sign anything if they happen to bring you an offer. Do not verbally accept or agree to anything. If for some reason we're surprised and there is an offer, just take the paperwork, confirm they'll email it to me, and then you and I will go over it."

If for some reason—

We're surprised—

Those two phrases might have sent him into a tailspin before, but today even though he hoped that they *were* surprised, that an offer might be made, he also knew it wouldn't break him, that his game wouldn't slip.

Because he was playing *his* game.

He wasn't his brothers or his dad or his grandfather.

He was Liam Williamson.

And that was enough.

"Got it," he told Ron. "Text me the details, but for now, I need to go."

"I—"

"Talk soon," he said and hung up to a surprised silence. Probably because that might have been the first time ever he'd gotten the last word, but also certainly because Ron wasn't used to his talking back in no-nonsense.

But Liam had absorbed a little Mia.

He could do cool confidence. He could do clipped and to the point.

He maybe couldn't do it *all* the time, but after hanging up the call with his agent and not feeling like a total fucking failure for the first time in ages, Liam knew he could find its place.

Fluff and charm most of the time. Firm and sharp at other moments.

It didn't have to be one or the other. *He* didn't have to be either, and that more than anything relaxed the final knots in his stomach.

The door opened, Mia's concerned face popping in through the gap.

He smiled at her. "Come here."

"What did they say?"

"They want to meet with me today," he said.

"Is that good or bad?" she asked, stepping close enough that he was able to snag her hand and tug her down into his lap.

"No clue." He wrapped his arm around her, burying his nose into her hair, inhaling the sweet scent of woman. "My agent doesn't know either. But at least I don't have long to wait."

She tilted her head up. "You don't seem worried."

"I'm not, J.B.," he said, pressing his lips to hers for a brief kiss. "For the first time in a long time, I'm not worried about the future."

"You're not?"

"No," he murmured. "Because my now is pretty great."

She snuggled in, hugged him tight. "Even though I just ordered you a T-shirt emblazoned with the word *Sugar?*"

Liam laughed. "Yes, J.B. Even though."

Her lips found his, holding him firmly, kissing him deeply, her tongue slipping into his mouth to tangle with his. It was hot. It was dirty. It was still laced with fluff. It also still made him go rock-hard, made him consider how difficult it would be to finagle himself a tour of her apartment overhead.

Not too difficult, he thought, based on the hard nipples pushing through the top of her *gi*, the dilated eyes, the chest rising and falling in rapid intervals.

"How about—"

The bell at the front of the studio tinkled, Blane's voice trickling through the open door. "Hello, Mia?" he called. "I'm sorry, I just realized I forgot to pay."

Liam's eyes were on her breasts, on those hard nipples that made his mouth water. She pushed off his lap, smacked him lightly when he slipped a hand through the opening. Such easy access. He just needed to untie one string—

"Stop it, you," she muttered, pushing his hands away. "I have to be presentable for my clients."

"Yoo-hoo!" Blane called. "I don't want to interrupt, but Mandy will kill me if—"

"I'll be right there," Mia called back.

"No, you won't," Liam said, standing, crowding into her. "Go away," he yelled. "Mia's on break until tonight."

"Liam," she hissed then her volume raised. "I—"

He kissed her, stifling the rest of her sentence, yanking her close, and what the hell, he allowed his hands to slip into the opening of that sexy uniform. Funny that, it really only did take one sharp tug to undo the tie, to have full access to the skin and woman beneath.

"I'll just leave a check here," Blane called.

Mia stiffened, started to pull away.

Liam let her go, or at least let her go enough so that he could tear his mouth from hers, so he could raise his voice, make sure it carried to Blane. "The keys are by the door, lock it on your way out!"

A gasp. An annoyed woman in his arms.

But Blane, who was certainly spying for the gossip train, who would definitely be reporting this incident to Mandy and company, just chuckled and said loud enough they could both hear, "I'll get them back to you later."

Parted lips, reddened cheeks, furious eyes.

Mia pulled out of his arms in a quick movement, spinning toward the door. But at the opening, she stopped, clutched the sides of her uniform together. "How did you—?" A sharp shake of her head before she peeked out. Then she sighed, turned back, plunking her hands on her hips. "Seriously?" she asked.

"You're beautiful."

She glared, crossed her arms. "Don't even try it."

And *seriously*, it wasn't his fault that the action plumped up her breasts, had his gaze dipping down, *staying* down.

She clapped her hands. "Eyes up here, buster."

Except the clapping made things jiggle and—

Another sigh as she brought a hand up, ran it slowly over the tops of her breasts, making his fingers tingle, his palms ache with the need to touch. Her tone softened, mouth curving up into a half-smile. "You're never going to stop pushing, never going to stop breaking my rules, are you?" she asked, stepping toward him, those curves so close and yet so far.

"No," he said, knowing it might have been better for his cock if he *had* lied, but unable to do so.

"Oh, Liam." She shook her head again, drifted closer. "What am I going to do with you?"

But then, before he could come up with a response that made her half-smile go full, made her laugh instead of glare, made her come to him and allow his hands to trace every inch of her . . . before he could do any of that, Mia took one step and launched herself into his arms.

It spoke more of her athletic ability than his that they both remained standing, but then her mouth dropped to his, her arms and legs wrapped tightly around him, and she kissed him until he stopped thinking about breaking rules and teasing.

She kissed him until he stopped thinking altogether.

She kissed him until *she* was the one coaxing him upstairs with an offer of a tour.

For the record, after her kiss had singed his nerve endings, had erased every bit of control, Liam considered it a fucking miracle that they made it up the stairs and through her front door.

Her entryway was really nice.

Also for the record, that was as much of her apartment as he saw.

TWENTY

MIA

She flicked off the lights to the studio, locked the door from the inside since Blane still had her keys, and glanced down at her cell for the hundredth time over the last few hours.

After the explosive sex in her front hallway—and she didn't think the table where she usually dropped her keys would ever recover—Liam's phone had buzzed with the time for his meeting with the Gold's owner, GM, and other staff, and it had been soon enough that he'd barely had time to run home, shower, and change into nice clothes. She'd gotten presentable in a hurry then walked him down to his car, kissing him goodbye and holding tight to his promise to call with news as soon as he was finished.

And he *had* called.

But it had been right in the middle of class, and she'd missed the call.

She'd called back as soon as she'd gotten a break, but then *he* hadn't picked up, and he also hadn't called again, and that had been hours ago.

And . . . now she was worried.

Really worried.

Mia considered her options as she went upstairs to change out of her karate uniform. She could stay here, remain in her safe little space and wait to hear from Liam. Or . . . her gaze fell onto the shell on her nightstand. The only physical item she had of her mother's, recovered from her body, given to her by the police officer who'd broken the news.

She remembered him showing up a few days afterward, a kind gray-haired man with gentle blue eyes. Mia had already been constricting then, locking down the pain of losing her mom and the guilt for her role in it. He'd asked if he could talk to her, had sat on the stairs leading down to the studio that was quiet, would remain quiet only for another day before her dad wrenched himself back into a brutal routine, dragging her alongside him.

But for that moment, he'd been quiet and lost in himself, and so Mia had gone with the officer, had sat down next to him on the stairs when he'd patted the worn wooden plank. He'd told her about losing his mom—in a car accident—handed her his card in case she needed to talk, and then he'd given her two things that had nearly shattered her.

One, a birthday card from the department with a gift certificate to a local clothing shop inside, saying, "It took me a long time to learn that I was allowed to celebrate." He'd set it in her lap, a gentle smile on his lips. "Don't be as dumb as I was."

The other was a plastic bag, the package inside wrapped carefully in tissue paper.

She'd cried when she had opened it.

A huge abalone shell. Cleaned of meat, and perhaps the most beautiful she'd ever seen, a pearly white iridescence with streaks of red and pale blue.

Because she'd known someone had found it on her mom and they'd realized how important it was, even though they couldn't have known that the shell would soon be the single thing she had left to remind Mia of her mother.

Or half of it anyway.

The officer had given her a squeeze, dried her tears, and told her to call.

Then he'd gone.

Mia hadn't called.

Because when she'd gone back inside to her bedroom, her father had walked by, had seen what she was holding, and he'd come out of his fog. His expression had been terrifying. He'd been furious, every muscle in his body locking as he burst toward her.

She'd forgotten her karate training.

Had cowered, hadn't stopped him when he'd ripped the items away from her. He'd torn the birthday card into shreds, thrown the certificate into the trash, along with the officer's number, but the shell . . . he'd launched that across the room with a fury that had her cowering on the bed.

One half had hit the wall, cracking, that beautiful iridescence flaking off and littering the carpet. The other half somehow managed to roll off a pile of laundry, to wedge itself beneath her desk and escape mostly unscathed. Mia hadn't found it until much later, until the apartment had been cleared out of her mother's things.

She'd hidden it deep in her closet.

But a few months ago, she'd stumbled on it, had set it on her nightstand.

So, maybe she hadn't been as stagnant as she'd first thought. Perhaps the change had been coming for a while, the trap winding tighter and tighter until it was finally sprung.

Until a man with a vein of sad had found a slice of happy because of her.

Until she'd let herself believe that it was possible to live not in a small box, but open and free . . . and more like how her mother had.

She ran her fingers along the smooth inside of the shell, the colors vibrant, the texture polished and as smooth as glass. Then she let them drift to the outside, to the rough, bumpy exterior that gave hardly a hint to what was inside. The metaphor for how she'd lived her life, for the juxtaposition of how her parents had been, wasn't lost on her.

The only difference was that she wanted some of that beauty for herself.

And Liam had shown her the way.

With teasing and slides, with scorching kisses and game-winning goals.

He'd given her the directions. She'd had to take those first steps.

She had. And she would keep taking them. So ultimately, it wasn't even a question of staying or going. She tugged on a sweat-shirt, picked up her apartment keys and phone. She would go to his place, be there when he got back and be there for him, regardless of the news.

He'd been her path.

Now she was going to return the favor.

Only . . . if she'd known what was awaiting her at Liam's place, she might not have been so determined.

In fact, strong, tough Mia might have chickened out.

TWENTY-ONE

LIAM

He stared at Pierre Barie, the very hands-off owner of the Gold—ostensibly because he'd bought the team after his son, Stefan, was made captain, and not being involved in the day-to-day operations was important for propriety's sake.

In reality, though, Pierre was a successful businessman, and he'd hired good people to run the organization.

He didn't need to be involved day to day.

Except, apparently, when it came to a Williamson.

Pierre had come into the boardroom a few minutes after the meeting had started, asking the GM Charlotte Harris and her assistant to give them a moment.

Now, he sat across the table from Liam and stared at him.

Silently.

Fun.

Eventually, Pierre sighed and slid a folder across the wooden surface. "You don't know, do you?"

Liam tried to figure out what the fuck that meant. Unable to do so, he settled on a simple, "No."

A nod toward the folder. "Take it."

Okay, this was suddenly feeling like an illegal arms deal, or perhaps entrapment, take the folder with dangerous information, triggering a swarm of federal agents that were going to burst out of nowhere, guns drawn, and demanding he get his ass on the floor. Or, since he had no knowledge of either of those things . . . Liam was merely delaying.

He reached for the folder.

Opened it.

And stopped breathing.

On the left side was an offer. A five-year contract with a reasonable amount of money based on his not ideal stats. He read quickly, knowing he would have time to look closer later, but he saw that even though the money was on the low end, there were bonuses if the team made it into the playoffs. Fair. At first glance, it seemed fair.

Then his eyes drifted to the right . . . and he saw it.

An email from his father.

An email sent to Pierre Barie, owner, businessman, the fucking boss of all Liam's bosses.

And his dad had emailed.

Worse, it wasn't a "Hi, how are you?" sort of message. It was terse. It was demanding . . . an offer for his son.

Liam shot to his feet, nausea burning the back of his throat.

He paced a few feet away, stopped and stared at the wall, trying to control the urge to punch his fist through it. What in the fuck had his dad been thinking? He wasn't Liam's agent or representative. This wasn't a place that mommies and daddies demanded things for their children. This was his work. His life. His—

He spun back, forced himself to sit back down at the table and take a deep breath. "No," he said, meeting Pierre's eyes. "I didn't know. I'm sorry. I'll make sure he doesn't contact you again." Liam closed the folder. "And I'll play hard for the rest of the season, do my best with the chance you guys gave me. I won't let you or them down." He slid the folder back and stood. "I'd hated hockey for a good while, but this team helped me find my love for it again. I won't let them down." He turned, readying himself to GTFO.

"Sit."

One sharp word and Liam obeyed without thinking.

Pierre didn't move to retrieve the folder, the paper having halted slightly beyond the halfway mark in its sliding trek. He remained silent, still staring.

Then he reached for the folder, stood, and went to the door.

A wave of disappointment washed over him. He wanted to run, to get away, to call his father and find out what in the fuck all he'd been thinking. But before he could do anything, Liam heard Pierre say, "Thank you for that. Please, come in."

Charlotte Harris and her assistant strode back into the room, pulling out chairs sitting down across the table from him, getting organized again. Charlotte was small and curvy with a laser-eyed focus and hair the color of autumn leaves turning from red to orange to brown.

But it was her smile that stole everyone's breath.

Wide, unfiltered, Hollywood-esque.

And incongruously, she flashed it at him right now.

"Thanks for coming in, Liam," she said. "We wanted to do this in person and since Mr. Barie is flying out tomorrow evening, we appreciate the last-minute meeting time." She shuffled through the papers in front of her, pulled out a stapled set. "I know your agent isn't here, so you'll need to take this and discuss —rest assured we've emailed him the details"—her eyes flicked to the side, caught her assistant's, who nodded in agreement—"you can take your time to look over the offer, but we've spoken with Bernard and the rest of the coaching staff. We're liking what you're doing for us on and off the ice—filling in for that charity event, putting in the extra time in the weight room and after practice." She passed the papers over to him. "You're a team player.

You have a good attitude and are well-liked. We want to find a way to keep you around."

There was that smile again, stealing his breath.

Except . . . this was his father's doing.

No matter the pretty words dressing up the situation, this wasn't anything to do with him.

This was a Williamson issue.

He opened his mouth—

A hand clamped onto his shoulder and startled, he glanced up at Pierre. The owner gave the slightest shake of his head, and Liam relaxed.

Charlotte didn't know. But that was one person. Who else had his dad influenced or reached out to or bullied? He loved his family, but they were complicated. They pushed and prodded and . . . demanded.

They could have easily twisted someone else's arm.

Charlotte's phone rang. "Excuse me," she said, stepping into the corner of the room and answering it.

"Just me," Pierre said quietly. "And I'm not a pushover. If you didn't earn it, the offer wouldn't be on the table, no matter who your father is."

"I—" He stood, dropped his voice. "I cannot believe he—" A shake of his head. "I'm sorry. That was absolutely uncalled for."

Pierre's mouth tipped at the corners. "Fathers sometimes do inexplicable things." A buzz of his phone and he glanced down. "I'm sure you'll have a chance to set him straight, sooner or later. That's my Diane. Charlotte!" he called and hitched his head toward the door, letting her know he was leaving. "Deep breath," he said, returning his gaze to Liam's. "Keep doing what you're doing. Let the rest of it be background noise."

"I promise I'll talk to him—"

"The great thing about email," Pierre said, "is that there's such a thing called filters. He can email all he wants, and I won't see it." With that and twinkling blue eyes, he left.

Liam stared after him for a long moment, the air frozen in his lungs.

Then he heard a voice raised and tuned back into the room, realizing he was beyond done with wasting time and energy and emotions on things he couldn't control. Charlotte was still talking on the phone and by the urgency and volume of her tone, Liam knew it was going to be a while. He stretched across the table, picked up the packet, and glanced her way.

She shot him an apologetic smile, but when he pointed to the chair, silently asking if she needed him to stay, she waved him off, covering the receiver with her hand. "Sorry," she called. "Thank you for coming in. Look that over and get back to us."

Liam nodded, said a quiet goodbye to her assistant, and left.

Oh, he intended to look the offer over.

Just as much as he intended to call his father and ensure that he would never—fucking *never*—intrude on Liam's life like that again.

His dad seemed to have forgotten Liam was a Williamson.

Strength. Stubbornness. A fiery fucking temper when provoked.

And let it be known, he had damn sure been provoked.

———

Fury still in every cell, but wanting to reassure the woman he loved, Liam dialed Mia's number as he walked out of the rink then glanced at his watch, realizing she was smack dab in the middle of her bank of classes, so he hung up, figuring he'd go back to his place, change, and head to her studio for a rousing edition of mat cleaning, contract reviewing, and phone calls to tell his father to never intervene in his life that way again.

Except, it didn't end up working out that way.

First, when he made it to his car, it was to see his tire had gone flat. He spent an inordinate amount of time trying to dislodge the lug nut but not ruining his suit before he managed to get it off, the tire changed, and back on his way.

In fact, he was so impatient to get to Mia that he couldn't even appreciate all of the innuendos and euphemisms inherent in the tire changing process—hello, dislodging nuts and getting off. Though, he did make a mental note that he was going to tease Mia with them later, if only to get her to glare at him. Then he'd give in to the temptation to kiss that glare away and . . .

"Focus, Liam," he muttered.

He needed to change. He needed to call his father. He needed to see Mia.

But, of course, by the time the tire was changed—he really should have just called AAA—it was now a weekday during rush hour, and he ended up inching his way along the freeway.

Way too fucking long later, Liam parked in the garage, took the elevator to his floor, and stepped off.

Then nearly stepped right back on.

Because his father was standing outside his condo, huge grin on his face. "I heard through the grapevine that you'd have good news today, son!" he boomed, striding toward him and squeezing Liam into a hug that stole the air from his lungs.

He'd liked it as a ten-year-old.

Fifteen years later and pissed at the interference in his life, Liam wasn't nearly as sanguine.

He pushed out of the embrace, resisting the urge to snap at his father, to control his boiling fury and not unleash on his father, who was looking proud, like he'd done something good, instead of intruding on Liam's life and making a fucking mess. His temper might be frayed, and he might be closer to that famous Williamson temper as he had at any point in his life.

But that wasn't him.

Breathe. Just breathe.

The firm order in Mia's voice had him doing just that.

This wasn't all his dad's fault. Liam had let his father interfere plenty of times over the years—too many times. Same as he'd spent too much energy and mental headspace letting his dad get him so twisted up with insights and help and suggestions that he'd barely been able to function. He'd never set any boundaries, so it probably didn't even cross his dad's mind to think that Liam would be anything less than grateful.

Hell, if he hadn't finally pulled his head out of his ass, thanks to Mia, he might have indeed been grateful. Embarrassed, but secretly glad that his dad had saved him once again.

But the thing was . . . Liam didn't need saving.

He could handle his own life, his own game, and that more than anything, was the most important thing he'd learned since coming to San Francisco.

Many years too late, but he'd gotten there anyway.

"Is that it?" His dad snagged the paper Liam held, as he let them into the condo, held the door for his father to trail him inside. "Let me see."

And Grant Williamson began reading, his face screwing up into a scowl as his eyes moved across the page. Liam ignored him, pushed the door closed, and peeled off his suit jacket.

"The money is shit," his dad said, tossing the paper down and pulling his cell out of his pocket. "I'm calling that lousy agent of yours right now—"

"Stop."

"—he should know better than to—"

"*Stop.*"

"—fuck with a Williamson. Two million a year. Your brothers got four times that, for fuck's sake."

Liam grabbed the cell from his hand, the contract from the other, and then he did something that had also taken him far too many years to do. He held his ground against his six-inch-taller, his fifty-pound-heavier father, and ordered him to, "Sit the fuck down, shut up, and listen to me for once in your fucking life."

And then while his dad stared at him in bewilderment, Liam started talking.

"I'm not you. I'm not Luke or Laich," he said. "I'm just *me*. I don't play hockey the same way as you, or them, or Grandpa. I probably will never be as good as you all were. I won't ever pull the same game numbers as Laich. Have the big hits like you and Luke." He sighed. "And until recently, I thought that made me weak or bad or . . . like I shouldn't be allowed to carry the name."

"Li—"

"No, Dad," he said. "Let me finish this. I know I should have said this sooner, but I always felt so damned inferior, and frankly, I was acting like a scared child when I should have been an adult. That's on me. But," he added when it looked like his dad might interject again, "what's on you is your inability to step back, to let us kids make mistakes."

"Why?" his father said. "Why in the hell would I want to let you make mistakes when I could make your life easier?"

Liam tossed his suit jacket on the back of the couch. "Because you didn't make things easier. You handicapped me, had me second and third and sometimes *fourth*-guessing what I should be doing on the ice. I was listening to my coaches, to my teammates, to you and Grandpa and Laich and Luke, and all the specialists you hired that I didn't ask for. I know you were trying to help, but I was so tied up with what everyone was saying that I couldn't play *my* game." He unbuttoned his cuffs, began rolling up his sleeves. "I should have told you to back off, but I was desperate, too. I wanted to be as good as the other Williamsons. But . . . I'm not."

"You've always been the best of us," his dad said stubbornly. "The best hands, the best skater, the best stats in peewees all the way up to juniors."

"And yet none of that matters in the big leagues. None of it matters *now*."

"You used to want my help."

"Did I?" Liam asked. "Or in that first season, when I was struggling with the pace, with the physicality, did I ask you to back off and let me figure things out on my own?" He hadn't stuck by that request, of course. His dad had pushed, Liam had been desperate to meet everyone's expectations . . . and he'd caved. He'd wanted to get better, to do well.

It was just that there were too many hands in the pot.

"I—"

"Dad," he interrupted. "*Please*. This is important. Think before you brush me off."

"You needed me."

A curl of disappointment wove through him, and Liam sighed, reaching for his jacket, tucking his dad's phone into his pocket. The last damned thing he needed right now was for his dad to start making further demands. This had to end, and if it meant launching multiple cells out of windows, or hacking into email accounts, then he'd do it.

"Please, listen to him."

The female voice had him glancing up to see Mia standing in the doorway, her face drawn, her eyes sad.

Liam must not have shut the door all the way.

He moved toward her, but his dad beat him there.

"Who are you?"

It was terse, snapped out, rivaling Mia's own tone from several weeks before. And Liam knew, instinctively, it was too terse, too sharp, to slicing for the Mia of today. Her steel was thinner after the memories, the conversations, and that fluff was too exposed.

It needed protecting or it would be destroyed.

She needed him.

That was the easy part.

Because she had him, and there was absolutely no way he was going to let his father bully the woman he loved. Even if her shoulders were straightening and she was gathering her armor. Even if she could protect herself.

This was his family. His dad. And he would not allow his woman to be hurt.

"First of all," he snapped, stepping between his father and Mia. "Absolutely fucking not." His dad opened his mouth, but

Liam glared him into silence. "You will *not* speak to *my* woman that way."

A soft gasp, fingers wrapped around his arm, a slender female body pressing into his back.

He sensed what she was telling him, that it was okay, that she didn't want to start any trouble.

Well, fuck that.

Liam had had his head in his ass with regards to his family for far too long.

His father narrowed his eyes. "I'll speak however—"

"I just told you everything I did, and you're still going to push?" Liam sighed, the disappointment heavy. "I just explained what I was feeling, now and in the past, and you're going to keep going along this path?"

"Liam," Mia said softly. "He's your dad."

He slipped his arm around her. "I know, J.B.," he said. "But this is important. This is my future, *our* future."

"Our?" his dad asked. "You've been here how long?" It was another snapped out question. "She's just after—"

"Stop right there if you ever want me to talk to you again."

It was said in a tone colder than Liam had ever remembered using, but fuck, he felt iced over, dissatisfied his dad wasn't listening, coldly furious that he'd dare discount what Mia and Liam had.

He was twenty-fucking-five.

He could make decisions about his life.

"You haven't bothered to pick up the phone as it is," his dad muttered. "Not since you came out here."

"And why do you think that is?" Liam asked.

Finally, *finally*, a slice of understanding seemed to cross his father's face, but before he could say anything, the phone in Liam's pocket rang—the one he'd taken from his dad.

He pulled it out, saw it was his mom calling, and put it on speaker.

"Hey, Mom," he said when it connected.

A sigh was his only response.

"Oh, Liam, baby," she said. "Tell me your father did not fly out there when I expressly told him to leave you alone."

"I—" his father began.

"No," she snapped, and his mom didn't get mad easily. For all the steel wool and brass balls, she was easy-going, usually let the boys do their own thing—it had been impossible in some ways to do anything aside from riding the tidal wave of Williamsons, he supposed. But she also definitely didn't use this particular tone unless shit was going to hit the fan. "We talked about this. I told you to leave him alone."

Terror chased away understanding, because his dad too knew that sparks were going to fly.

"Baby—"

"Grant."

That was it. Just *Grant.*

Then a sigh, her tone going frigid. "We talked about this after I spoke with Liam a few weeks ago, after *you* spoke to Liam and he asked you to give him space." A pause. "You promised me you'd respect that."

"Baby—"

"Get your ass on the next plane home," she snapped, "and leave Liam to his life. You can't control the world or the goals that go into the net, *or* your son." A beat, voice warming. "Love you, Liam. I'll talk to you soon."

Then she hung up.

And left silence in her wake.

Twenty-Two

MIA

She stood next to Liam, watching the man she'd wanted to despise upon meeting him. But now he was there, family plain in his striking gray eyes that were the same as Liam's eyes.

The same pain that had been in Liam's when she'd first met him.

"I failed you," his dad whispered.

"What?" Liam frowned.

"I wasn't there much when you boys were growing up, even less so for you."

Mia's breath caught, and she tried to slip away, intending to go down the hall to the bedroom to give them some privacy, but when she shifted, Liam just held her more tightly against him.

So, she stayed.

"You can't control where you were traded, Dad."

Sad gray eyes. "I know."

"I also never resented you playing," Liam said. "You loved it, and when you were home, you were fun." He chuckled, the tension leaving his body. "Why do you think my friends were always at the house? You were always driving Mom crazy with your antics."

"I had to make up for it," his dad said.

"There was nothing to make up for." Liam played his fingers through her hair. "It was your job, and it was undoubtedly cool to have a hockey player dad."

"I spent more time with Luke and Laich."

"I was fine," Liam said. "I didn't need that extra time."

"And the pressure?"

"Well, that's always been there," Liam said. "We're Williamsons, riding Grandpa's legacy, riding yours. That pressure isn't going away, so I'm going to do my best to figure out how to manage it better."

Another flash of sad. "And I'm not helping."

Liam stiffened. "Dad."

A sigh. "Is this your way of telling me to mind my business?"

"No," Liam said. "*This* is me telling you to mind your own business. Again." He shook his head. "This is me telling you not to worry if I have a bad game. Demanding that you let me make my own way, whether it's a spiral downward or a climb upward."

"I'm not sure I can do that."

Mia couldn't be quiet any longer. She didn't quite understand the man's guilt or get why he was pushing this so hard. But she understood her own guilt, her own loss, and she didn't want these two men to not be able to find a common ground. "Do it," she said. "Find a way. Be the father your son deserves, not the one that your guilt is pushing you to be."

Cool gray eyes on hers. "And what do you know about guilt, little girl?"

She lifted her chin. "Probably more than *you'll* ever know, old man."

Not the politest remark to the father of the man she loved, but she'd had more than her fair share of pain and regrets over the last decade, and she didn't want Liam to miss out on a dad who might be pushy, but who also very clearly cared for his son.

She waited for a cool remark, for a snapped reply.

Instead, she got a small smile, gray eyes flicking toward Liam. "I like her, son."

"I knew you would."

His father sighed then stuck out his hand. "We're doing this all sorts of backward, but I'm Grant. It's nice to meet you."

She shook it. "Mia. It's nice to meet you, too."

They stood there awkwardly for a moment then she stepped away from Liam. "I should let you two talk—"

"Oh, no," Grant said. "My ass has got to get on a plane." His eyes twinkled. "I'm already in too much hot water with the wife to risk not following orders. Plus, I think you lovebirds could use some privacy without an *old man* ruining the fun."

Mia groaned. "I'm not going to live that down, am I?"

"I've already ordered him a shirt emblazoned with the name," Liam said dryly.

She lifted a brow. "How? With your superpowers?"

"Precisely. Plus, it'll go with the one you ordered for me." He kissed the top of her head then looked up at his dad. "I'd say that it was a nice surprise . . ."

Grant snorted. "Reading you loud and clear, son," he said, palms out. "No more surprise visits. No phone calls. I can promise that much."

"Phone calls are okay."

Surprise on his father's face. "Yeah?"

"Yeah." Liam chuckled. "So long as they're not about hockey."

"Roger that." Grant stepped forward, hugged his son tightly, then he surprised Mia by turning and hugging her, albeit much more gently. "Thanks for kicking my ass, L.G."

She leaned back, studied mischievous gray eyes. "What's with you and your son and abbreviations?"

Grant frowned. "What?"

"What does L.G. stand for?"

A grin. "Little Girl."

She sighed, sent her gaze toward the ceiling. "Oh, boy."

"What's your abbreviation?" he asked his son.

She glanced down, saw that Liam was smiling. "J.B."

Grant laughed. "Yeah. I could see it."

"See what?" she exclaimed, losing patience. "What the hell does it mean?"

Another laugh, Grant clapping his hand on Liam's shoulder. "I'll leave you to deal with that one." His chest lifted and fell on a quiet breath. "And . . . I'm sorry."

Mia forgot about her annoyance of the phrase *I'll leave you to deal with that one*, and had to blink rapidly so that no pesky tears escaped. Hell, these Williamson men were turning her into a watering pot.

Especially when Liam hugged his dad again and said, "It's okay."

She sniffed, two pairs of identical eyes coming to her, and they broke apart, Liam moving to her side, Grant heading for the door and saying, "Don't worry, Li. I won't take that as permission to start up again."

"See that you don't, Dad."

Grant opened the door. "I'll call you tomorrow!"

Liam stiffened.

"Kidding!" Grant stepped out, the door starting to close behind him. "Love you, son," were the last words that came before the panel slid shut.

She turned to the man who'd so effectively stolen her heart and cupped his cheek. "I'm so proud of you."

"Thank you." A brush of his lips, a smile in the touch. "Also, I love you."

Warmth. God, this man made her feel so warm, so complete, so . . . loved. But she also wasn't about to let him off the hook.

"Nice try," she muttered. "Now tell me, *Sugar*, what the hell does J.B. mean?"

His father had known in an instant. How? Was it some pop

culture reference she didn't get? Or an inside joke with the Williamson clan? Or—

Firm lips on hers, fingers sliding into her hair. "Wouldn't you rather hear about the meeting?"

No. Yes. Dammit. *Yes.*

She made a face, knowing that stumbling onto the conversation Liam had been having with his dad, the door having slid open when she'd lifted her hand to knock, had distracted her. The contract was more important than the nickname, though she made a mental note to Google judiciously later.

"Yes," she said begrudgingly.

In response, he handed her a packet of papers.

Brows drawn together, she began reading. The first sentence had her eyebrows relaxing, the next her lips curving up, the rest . . . she looked up, pulse pounding, heart squeezing. "Five years?"

He nodded. "Yeah, J.B. Five years."

She hugged him, throwing her arms around his neck and squeezing tightly. "Damn," she said. "I guess I'm going to have to get used to having you around."

Liam snorted, wrapped his own arms tightly around her. "Got enough mats for me to clean?"

"I'm sure I can scrounge a few up."

Another laugh. "I love you."

"I love you, too."

And then, with the papers that ensured his future would be bright in the Golden State crunched between them, Liam scooped her up into his arms and kissed her.

He kissed her until her head spun.

He kissed her until *his* head spun, apparently.

He kissed her until his legs gave way and he plunked down onto his ass, right there in the front hallway of the condo.

Fitting that.

Even more fitting was him teasing her much later, when he was carrying her naked and pleasured body into the bedroom, saying, "What's it with you and entryways?"

And because her mom was in her heart, because this man had made it possible for her to open that heart, it was just as fitting to tease him back, "What's with you ending up on your ass around me all the time? I mean, it's a really nice ass, but—ack!"

He tossed her on the bed, followed her down, and proceeded to show her exactly how much he liked *her* ass.

And her. Just her.

Just her heart, her mind, her body.

She was enough. For herself. For him. For her happy future.

But she still didn't find out what J.B. stood for.

EPILOGUE

PART ONE

MIA

They'd lost.

It was heartbreaking. As the series had progressed, she'd just kept thinking they would turn it around, they would get that goal, come from behind, sneak out a win.

But all of that thinking and hoping hadn't changed anything.

It was the second round of the playoffs, and the Gold were out.

Former champions to the end of the season.

"Damn," she murmured, waiting until the crowd began clearing out of the Gold Mine before making her way to the PT Suite. She knew her way now. Mandy had even gotten her a pass, saying she had to come see her after every game before she went up to the Family Suite.

As much as the other women had welcomed her, Mia felt more comfortable with Mandy.

Maybe it was their shared adoration of book to movie adaptions, or maybe . . . it was just that listening to Mandy banter and order people around reminded Mia of her mother.

Either way, she'd gotten very good at making Mandy's special bruise cream.

Which had definitely been in high demand this late in the season and with the various injuries the team was dealing with.

Brit out with a dislocated shoulder.

Blane playing with a broken foot.

Liam had a hairline fracture in his wrist.

Kevin had missed two games due to a concussion.

And that didn't even include Coop or Logan or any of the rest of the guys, who were all playing with different levels of discomfort.

"I suppose I can't call karate the real sport any longer," she said, walking into the PT Suite and hugging Mandy. "Your man kicked ass even with that foot."

Mandy smiled sadly. "I'm so mad at him for playing."

"You have all summer to doctor him up."

A pout, but then Mandy squeezed her again. "This is always the worst part. It's over, and they didn't win." She sniffed.

Mia didn't point out that all the teams, but one, was in or would be in the same position. She was just as disappointed, albeit for Liam rather than for Blane and the rest of the guys.

Most of them had won the Cup.

Liam hadn't.

"There will be more opportunities."

Mandy nodded, pulling back, and swiped a finger under each eye. "Ignore me," she said. "I'm hormonal."

Mia lifted a brow.

To which Mandy clamped a hand over her mouth and glanced around. "Tell me no one heard that," she hissed. "Blane doesn't even know yet."

A grin turned up the corners of her mouth and earned her a swat from Mandy. But when Mia kept grinning, Mandy turned around and saw the man standing behind her. Tall, pretty, and sweaty, he tugged Mandy into his arms. He placed his hand over her belly. "Really?"

She nodded. "I just found out before the game."

Mia looked away when Blane dropped his head, whispered something in Mandy's ear that made her cheeks flush bright red, but as touched as she was by the scene, it had nothing on the man who was standing in the doorway.

She went to him, threw her arms around his neck. "I'm sorry, Sugar."

A squeeze, a soft chuckle. "Digging the knife in, J.B.?"

Pulling back, she plunked her hands on her hips. "Well, you haven't given up the goods now, have you?" she asked pertly before softening her tone. "Are you—"

"I *hope* to God he's given up the goods by now," Coop said, pushing by them.

"No," Brit said, inching by them in a suit, her arm still in a sling from the injury. "Liam's too nice. He's probably waiting for a diamond ring and flowers."

"Are you?" she asked Liam.

"Am I—?"

Kevin slid through the door and Liam cursed, tugged them to the side so they were out of the flow of traffic.

"Am I what?" he asked, able to get the question out the second time.

"Waiting for a diamond ring and flowers?" she asked, made to head back to the door, to step through it. "I can go get you some, if you need it."

A roll of pretty gray eyes. "Smartass."

"Your fault."

"True."

"Are you okay?"

He nodded. "Yeah, sweetheart, I am." Then his gaze flicked to the right. "Mandy, I hate to interrupt the love fest, but do you have it?"

Mia glanced to the side, saw Mandy jump out of Blane's arms and retrieve a small box from a drawer. So tossed it to Liam, who caught it, and handed it to Mia. "Open it."

Her breath caught. It wasn't the right size for a ring, and it was too soon for that anyway. They'd discussed a future, decided that even though they'd moved from like to love quickly, it made sense to enjoy their time together.

Or was she wrong?

She didn't know jewelry. It *could* be a ring box.

Had he changed his mind?

And if he had, what would her answer be?

Lips on her ear. "Stop thinking so hard," he murmured, tearing off the paper, "and just open it."

Shaking fingers fumbled with the lid.

And then she saw inside.

Her gaze met his, lips curving.

It wasn't a ring. It was *better*. A delicate gold necklace with letter charms that spelled out a word. But not just any word. They spelled out his nickname for her. She ran her fingers over each letter, all ten of them. "*That's* what J.B. stands for?"

Liam grinned, bending to nuzzle at her throat. "Yup." A nip. "I thought it was fitting."

Mandy snatched the box from her hands, causing them to jump apart.

"Jawbreaker?" She smacked Liam. "What the hell? That's not an engagement ring like you said."

"No, it's not." A beat and she turned back to see he'd shifted down to one knee, was holding up a smaller box. "But *this* is."

Mia's heart leaped.

She knew what her answer would be, knew it would have never been anything else. Fingers along his jaw, palm cupped his cheek. "Always have to push, don't you?"

"You wouldn't want me any other way," he said, turning his head to kiss her palm.

A nod, her eyes filling with tears. "That's true."

"So, is it a yes?" Mandy asked, impatience in every syllable.

"It's a yes," Mia said.

Liam was on his feet in a second, and she was in his arms in the next, his mouth descending, his lips on hers. And just like that, this man she loved with her whole heart had taken sad and turned it into happy.

That was *his* superpower.

And Mia knew she was so damned lucky to have saved him from becoming a San Franciscan pancake.

Because he'd saved her right back.

CHARLOTTE

"Damn," she muttered, sitting down at her computer and slipping off her heels.

They'd lost.

Her first year as GM and she hadn't been able to get the job done.

She made a show of checking her emails, of sending a few notes to their big sponsors and to the board, thanking them for their support of the team and for a good season, but in reality, all she could think was that she'd lost.

Fuck, she hated losing.

Had hated it from the first time she'd lost the Chubby Bunny contest when she'd been a Daisy at Girl Scout camp.

She still hated it.

Hell, she'd picked a career whose main focus was building an organization that could win as much as possible, that's how much she hated losing.

What she hated even more?

Being the only female GM in the league and losing in the second round of the playoffs.

God, was it too much to ask for the Cup, just one more time?

Probably.

She sighed. The Gold had won the previous season and two before that. Two out of four was still a hell of a record.

It just . . . wasn't her record.

"Fuck," she muttered, shutting down her computer and shoving her feet back into her heels. Since that was basically akin to torture after wearing them all day, she was not happy when the knock came at the door, and called, "Come in," while continuing to pack her bag.

If only she'd known who was on the other side.

But unfortunately, she couldn't see through walls.

So when the man opened the door and pushed inside her office, Charlotte didn't have the chance to gird her loins.

Like she'd been doing all season.

Because—also unfortunately—she'd made the decision early on in her tenure to bring Logan Walker to the Gold. He was ferociously talented at defense. Big and strong and fast, he'd made an excellent replacement for Stefan Barie this season.

He was also her ex.

And just being in the same room with him had her body remembering why he was her ex.

Cocky smile.

Sexy body.

Flaming chemistry.

But not ready to settle down.

So, as one might expect, take a young Charlotte Harris, add in one cocky, sexy, scorching Logan Walker, and the result had been a broken heart.

Not just broken. Shattered.

The pieces scattered to the four corners of the earth.

In case anyone was wondering, young intern meets rookie hockey player did not make for a happy ending.

But that was fine. It was better. She'd gotten tougher and stronger and she'd promised herself that she would never let anyone in that deeply again, never make herself as vulnerable.

"I knew you'd be like this," he said, and fuck if that gruff voice didn't send a shiver down her spine.

She ignored him, continued packing her computer bag. He'd

get to the point, or he wouldn't, and she'd keep doing what she did best. Putting her head down and charging forward.

"Always hate losing."

His voice was closer now, but she still didn't look up, even though the spicy scent of his aftershave was drifting through the air, tickling her nose, making her fingers clench on her bag.

No.

Ignoring him and his sexy body, his sexy voice, his sexy scent, she packed a bunch of shit she didn't need, all so she didn't have to look at him.

She reached for a pad of sticky notes—

Warm, calloused hands on hers.

"You don't need a sixth pad," he said, that voice curling over her shoulders, sending heat between her thighs.

She jerked away. "You don't know *what* I need," she snapped.

A sigh. A hip resting on her desk. "Why did you pick me up, Char?"

Charlotte swallowed, zipped her bag closed—*with* the sixth pad of sticky notes, thank her very much—and forced herself to meet his gaze. "You were the best man for the position. We needed solid D. You brought it."

Green eyes, such a rich emerald they almost looked black, locked on hers. "That's it?"

"That's it." She picked up her bag. "I'm tired, so I'm sure you're doubly so." She started to round the desk but stopped, knowing she needed to be professional. Not only was she the first female GM, but she'd set a standard for herself when she'd joined the organization. "You played well this season and especially during the playoffs."

A nod. "Thanks."

That confused her. Before, his cocky would have taken over. Today, he seemed modest? Come to think of it, she hadn't seen a lot of cocky this season, at least not when it came to his game play. But it had been eight years since they'd been alone in a room together, she supposed things had to have changed.

Not that it mattered.

Things had changed on her front, too.

She wasn't the naïve little girl anymore.

She was strong and powerful and had a whole lot of people depending on her.

"If you'll excuse me." Charlotte pointed to the door. "We should be going."

"Your feet hurt."

Her brows drew together. "What?"

Logan nodded at her feet, clad in a lovely pair of heels that while beautiful, were also the equivalent of bear traps—and if that wasn't the perfect metaphor for the man in front of her, she didn't know what was.

"Those heels hurt you." His head tilted to the side. "Why do you wear them?"

She scoffed. "None of your fucking business, Walker."

A smile—slow and hot and sliding like silk over her breasts, her stomach, between her thighs. "I knew you'd say that."

"I—"

He held up a box, pushed it into her hands when she stepped back. "Open it," he said, voice dropping and joining that silk of his smile to dip between her legs. "If you think you can handle it."

And then he was gone, the door closing behind him, leaving her with a heavy ass bag packed with who knew what, aching feet, and a box in her hands.

A box given on a challenge.

A box he knew she'd open.

Because Charlotte Harris didn't give in or back down. She liked that even less than she liked losing.

So, she opened the lid.

And instantly knew she was in trouble.

———

Thank you for reading! I hope you loved meeting Mia and Liam! The next book in the Gold Hockey series is CHARGING.
Once upon a time she'd been an intern.
Once upon a time *he'd* been a rookie.

GET CHARGING HERE NOW>

And if you enjoyed CENTERED, you'll love the sexy, sweet, and close-knit Breakers Hockey crew. <u>The first book in the series, BROKEN, is now live!</u>

The more she falls for Stefan, the more she risks her career...
Don't miss the first Gold Hockey book. The over 400 five-star-reviewed BLOCKED is FREE!

"Off-the-charts hot, smexy scenes with one of the best book boyfriends I have come across!" —Amazon reviewer

DOWNLOAD BLOCKED FOR FREE >

I so appreciate your help in spreading the word about my books, including sharing with friends! Please leave a review on your favorite book site!
You can also join my Facebook group, the Fabinators, for exclusive giveaways and sneak peeks of future books.

SIGN UP FOR ELISE FABER'S NEWSLETTER HERE:
https://www.elisefaber.com/newsletter

———

Want a free bonus story? Hate missing Elise's new releases? Love contests, exclusive excerpts and giveaways?
Then signup for Elise's newsletter here!
https://www.elisefaber.com/newsletter

———

And join Elise's fan group, the Fabinators https://www.facebook.com/groups/fabinators for insider information, sneak peaks at new releases, and fun freebies! Hope to see you there!

Gold Hockey Series

Gold Hockey **(all stand alone)**
Blocked
Backhand
Boarding
Benched
Breakaway
Breakout
Checked
Coasting
Centered
Charging
Caged
Crashed
A Gold Christmas
Cycled
Caught
Cap

Gold Hockey

Did you miss any of the Gold Hockey books?
Find information about the full series here.
Or keep reading for a sneak peek into each of the books below!

Blocked
Gold Hockey Book #1
Get your copy at https://www.elisefaber.com/blocked

Brit

The first question Brit always got when people found out she played ice hockey was *"Do you have all of your teeth?"*

The second was *"Do you, you know, look at the guys in the locker room?"*

The first she could deal with easily—flash a smile of her full set of chompers, no gaps in sight. The second was more problematic. Especially since it was typically accompanied by a smug smile or a coy wink.

Of course she looked. *Everybody* looked once. Everyone snuck a glance, made a judgment that was quickly filed away and shoved deep down into the recesses of their mind.

And she meant *way* down.

Because, dammit, she was there to play hockey, not assess her teammates' six packs. If she wanted to get her man candy fix, she could just go on social media. There were shirtless guys for days filling her feed.

But that wasn't the answer the media wanted.

Who cared about locker room dynamics? Who gave a damn whether or not she, as a typical heterosexual woman, found her fellow players attractive?

Yet for some inane reason, it *did* matter to people.

Brit wasn't stupid. The press wanted a story. A scandal. They were desperate for her to fall for one of her teammates—or better yet the captain from their rival team—and have an affair that was worthy of a romantic comedy.

She'd just gotten very good at keeping her love life—as nonexistent as it was—to herself, gotten very good at not reacting in any perceptible way to the insinuations.

So when the reporter asked her the same set of questions for the thousandth time in her twenty-six years, she grinned—showing off those teeth—and commented with a sweetly innocent "Could've sworn you were going to ask me about the coed showers." She waited for the room-at-large to laugh then said, "Next question, please."

–Get your copy at https://www.elisefaber.com/blocked

Backhand
Gold Hockey Book #2
Get your copy at https://www.elisefaber.com/backhand

SARA

"Sorry I messed up your sketch," he rumbled.

She nibbled on the side of her mouth, biting back a smile. "Sorry I stole your hand for so long."

He shrugged. "My mom's an artist. I get it."

Well, there went her battle with the smile. Her lips twitched and her teeth came out of hiding. If there was one thing that Sara had, it was her smile. It had been her trademark in her competition days.

Which were long over.

Her mouth flattened out, the grin slipping away. Time to go, time to forget, to move on, to rebuild. "Thanks," she said and extended a hand.

Then winced and dropped it when her ribs cried out in protest.

"You okay?" he asked, head tilting, eyes studying her.

"Fine." And out popped her new smile. The fake one. Careful of her aching side, she shrugged into her backpack. "I've got to go." She turned, ponytail flapping through the hair to land on her opposite shoulder.

"That—" He touched her arm. "Wait. I *know* I know you."

She froze. That was the second time he'd said that, and now they were getting into dangerous territory. Recognition meant . . . no. She couldn't.

There had been a time when *everyone* had known her. Her face on Wheaties boxes, her smile promoting toothpaste and credit cards alike.

That wasn't her life any longer.

"Thanks again. Bye." She started to hurry away.

"Wait." A hand dropped on to her shoulder, thwarting her escape, and she hissed in pain.

"Sorry," he said, but he didn't release her. Instead, he shifted his grip from her aching shoulder down to her elbow and when she didn't protest, he exerted gentle pressure until Sara was facing him again. "It's just that know I *know* you."

No. This wasn't happening.

"You're Sara Jetty."

Her body went tense.

Oh God. This was *so* happening.

"It's me." He touched his chest like she didn't know he was talking about himself, and even as she was finally recognizing the color of his eyes, the familiar curve of his lips and line of his jaw, he said the worst thing ever, "Mike Stewart."

Oh *shit*.

—Get your copy at https://www.elisefaber.com/backhand

Boarding
Gold Hockey Book #3
Get your copy at https://www.elisefaber.com/boarding

MANDY

Hockey players had the *best* asses.

No pancake bottoms, these men—and *women*—could fill out a pair of jeans. She wanted to squeeze it, to nibble it, bounce a dime—

Mandy dropped her chin to her chest, losing sight of the Sorting Hat cupcakes she'd been pondering.

Blane with his yummy ass had a unique way of distracting her.

No, it wasn't even distraction, per se. He had *always* been able to get under her skin.

And that was very, very bad for her.

"Ugh," she said, tossing her phone onto her desk and standing, knowing that she wouldn't be able to sit still now.

Nope, she needed about forty laps in the pool and a good hard fu—

Run, her mind blurted, almost yelling at the mental voice of her inner devil. *A good hard run.*

Unfortunately, the cajoling tone wasn't completely drowned out. *Some sexy horizontal time with Blane would be more fun—*

But the rest of the enticing words were lost as the roar of the crowd suddenly penetrated through the layers of concrete. Her stomach twisted. Mandy could tell, even before her eyes made it to the television, that it wasn't in celebration of a goal or a good hit either.

This was fury, a collective of outrage.

She was on her feet the moment she saw the prone form lying so still face down on the ice.

Her gut twisted when she spotted the curving line of a numeral two on the back of the player's jersey.

"Not him," she said and the words were familiar, a sentiment she had whispered, had *prayed* a thousand times before. She needed the camera angle to shift, for her to be able to see more clearly *who* was hurt. "Not him."

Then Dr. Carter was on the ice and the player moved slightly, rolling away from the camera, giving a full shot of his back and the matching twos adorning his jersey.

Fuck. Not him. Not Blane.

And that was when she saw the pool of blood.

—Get your copy at https://www.elisefaber.com/boarding

Benched
Gold Hockey Book #4
Get your copy at https://www.elisefaber.com/benched

MAX

He started up the car, listening and chiming in at the right places as Brayden talked all things video game.

But his mind was unfortunately stuck on the fact that women were not to be trusted.

He snorted. Brit—the Gold's goalie and the first female in the NHL—and Mandy—the team's head trainer—would smack him around for that sentiment, so he silently amended it to: *most* women were not to be trusted.

There. Better, see?

Somehow, he didn't think they'd see.

He parked in the school's lot, walked Brayden in, and received the appropriate amount of scorn from the secretary for being thirty minutes late to school, then bent to hug Brayden.

"I'll pick you up today," he said.

Brayden smiled and hugged him tightly. Then he whispered something in his ear that hit Max harder than a two-by-four to the temple.

"If you got me a new mom, we wouldn't be late for school."

"Wh-what?" Max stammered.

"Please, Dad? Can you?"

And with that mind fuck of an ask, Brayden gave him one more squeeze and pushed through the door to the playground, calling, "Love you!" over his shoulder.

Then he was gone, and Max was standing in the office of his son's school struggling to comprehend if he had actually just heard what he'd heard.

A new mom?

Fuck his life.

—Get your copy at https://www.elisefaber.com/benched

Breakaway
Gold Hockey Book #5
Get your copy at https://www.elisefaber.com/breakaway

BLUE

"Thanks for the ride."

"Try not to go out and get a fresh bimbo to ride tonight. I hear STIs on are the rise in the city."

Blue sighed, turned back to face her. "Really?"

She shrugged, smirk teasing the edges of her mouth, drawing his focus to the lushness of her lips. "Just watching out for Max's teammate."

He rolled his eyes. "Not hardly."

"Okay, how about I'm trying to prevent you from spreading STIs to the female populace."

"I'm clean, and I'm smart," he told her. "Condoms all the way."

"Ew."

Except there was something about the way she said it that made Blue stiffen and take notice. Because . . . he stared into her eyes, watched as the pale blue darkened to royal, saw her lips part, and her suck in a breath.

Holy shit.

"You're attracted to me."

Her jaw dropped. "No fucking way," she said, too quickly, pink dancing on the edges of her cheekbones. "You're delusional."

Blue got close.

Real close.

Anna licked her lips.

And fuck it all, he kissed that luscious mouth.

—Breakaway, https://www.elisefaber.com/breakaway

Breakout
Gold Hockey Book #6
Get your copy at https://www.elisefaber.com/breakout

PR-REBECCA

A fucking perfect hockey fairy tale.

Shaking her head, because she knew firsthand that fairy tales didn't exist outside of rom-coms and occasionally between alpha sports heroes and their chosen mates, Rebecca slipped through the corridor and stepped onto the Gold's bench.

Lots of dudes in suits—of both the boardroom *and* the hockey variety—were hugging.

On the ice. Near the goals. On the bench.

It was a proverbial hug-fest.

And she was the cynical bitch who couldn't enjoy the fact

that the team she was with had just won the biggest hockey prize of them all.

"I knew you'd be like this."

Rebecca turned her focus from Brit, who was skating with the huge silver cup, to the man—no, to the *boy* because no matter how pretty and yummy he was, Kevin was still a decade younger than her—leaning oh so casually against the boards.

"Nice goal," she told him.

A shrug. "Blue made a nice pass."

And dammit, the fact that he wasn't an arrogant son of a bitch made her like him more.

She nodded at the cup. "You should go have your turn."

"I'll get mine," he said with another shrug.

She frowned, honestly confused. "You don't want—"

Suddenly he was in front of her on the bench, towering over her even though she was wearing her four-inch power heels. "You know what I want?"

Rebecca couldn't speak. Her breath had whooshed out of her in the presence of all that sweaty, hockey god-ness. Fuck he was pretty and gorgeous and . . . so fucking masculine that her thighs actually clenched together.

She wanted to climb him like a stripper pole.

"Do you?" he asked again when her words wouldn't come. "Want to know what I want?"

She nodded.

He bent, lips to her ear. "You, babe," he whispered. "I. Want. You."

Then he straightened and jumped back onto the ice, leaving her gaping after him like she had less than two brain cells in her skull.

The worst part?

She wanted him, too.

Had wanted him since the moment she'd laid eyes on the sexy as sin hockey god.

"Trouble," she murmured. "I'm in *so* much fucking trouble."

—Breakout, https://www.elisefaber.com/breakout

Checked

Gold Hockey Book #7

Get your copy at https://www.elisefaber.com/checked

"Rebecca."

She kept walking.

She might work with Gabe, but she sure as heck wasn't on speaking terms with him. He'd dismissed her work, ignored her contribution to the team. He'd made her feel small and unimportant and—

She kept walking.

"*Rebecca.*"

Not happening. Her car was in sight, thank fuck. She beeped the locks, reached for the handle.

He caught her arm.

"Baby—"

"I am *not* your baby, and you don't get to touch me." She ripped herself free, started muttering as she reached for the handle of her car again. "You don't even like me."

He stepped close, real close. Not touching her, not pushing the boundary she'd set, and yet he still got really freaking close. Her breath caught, her chin lifted, her pulse picked up. "That. Is. Where. You're. Wrong."

She froze.

"What?"

His mouth dropped to her ear, still not touching, but near enough that she could feel his hot breath.

"I like you, Rebecca. Too fucking much."

Then he turned and strode away.

—Checked, https://www.elisefaber.com/checked

Coasting
Gold Hockey Book #8
Get your copy at https://www.elisefaber.com/coasting

Coop

Without thinking, he caught her arm.

"You're not okay."

She shuddered to a stop when he touched her, not fighting the grip, chin dropping to her chest. "No," she said, "you're right. I'm not okay."

"Who was on the phone?" he asked gently.

Her jaw went tight. "My ex."

Fury blazed through him. "Did he hurt you?" he growled.

A shake of her head. "Not like you're thinking." She sucked in a breath. "He broke my heart."

Coop's own heart gave a twinge. "I'm sorry, Calle. That's—"

"Fucking stupid." Another tear joined the first, dripping down the pale skin of her cheek.

"It's not stupid to have loved someone," he said gently.

Her eyes went fierce. "It's incredibly stupid when the person who supposedly loves you right back doesn't give a damn that you're pregnant."

His jaw fell open. He knew it did.

But Calle? Even, gentle *Calle* had gotten knocked up and—

"Yup," she said, brushing by him. "See? Really *fucking* stupid."

And without another word, she disappeared into the rink.

—Coasting, https://www.elisefaber.com/coasting

Also by Elise Faber

Billionaire's Club (all stand alone)

Bad Night Stand

Bad Breakup

Bad Husband

Bad Hookup

Bad Divorce

Bad Fiancé

Bad Boyfriend

Bad Blind Date

Bad Wedding

Bad Engagement

Bad Bridesmaid

Bad Swipe

Bad Girlfriend

Bad Best Friend

Bad Billionaire's Quickies

Gold Hockey (all stand alone)

Blocked

Backhand

Boarding

Benched

Breakaway

Breakout

Checked

Coasting

Centered

Charging

Caged

Crashed

A Gold Christmas

Cycled

Caught

Cap

Breakers Hockey (all stand alone)

<u>Broken</u>

<u>Boldly</u>

<u>Breathless</u>

<u>Ballsy</u>

<u>Bewitched</u>

Love, Action, Camera (all stand alone)

Dotted Line

Action Shot

Close-Up

End Scene

Meet Cute

Love After Midnight (all stand alone)

Rum And Notes

Virgin Daiquiri

On The Rocks

Sex On The Seats

***Life Sucks Series* (all stand alone)**

Train Wreck

Hot Mess

Dumpster Fire

Clusterf*@k

FUBAR (March 29,2022)

***Roosevelt Ranch Series* (all stand alone, series complete)**

Disaster at Roosevelt Ranch

Heartbreak at Roosevelt Ranch

Collision at Roosevelt Ranch

Regret at Roosevelt Ranch

Desire at Roosevelt Ranch

***Phoenix Series* (read in order)**

Phoenix Rising

Dark Phoenix

Phoenix Freed

***Phoenix: Lex Tal Chronicles* (rereleasing soon, stand alone, Phoenix world)**

From Ashes

In Flames

To Smoke

KTS Series

Riding The Edge

Crossing The Line

Leveling The Field

Scorching The Earth

Cocky Heroes World

Tattooed Troublemaker

ABOUT THE AUTHOR

USA Today bestselling author, Elise Faber, loves chocolate, Star Wars, Harry Potter, and hockey (the order depending on the day and how well her team -- the Sharks! -- are playing). She and her husband also play as much hockey as they can squeeze into their schedules, so much so that their typical date night is spent on the ice. Elise changes her hair color more often than some people change their socks, loves sparkly things, and is the mom to two exuberant boys. She lives in Northern California. Connect with her in her Facebook group, the Fabinators or find more information about her books at www.elisefaber.com.

f facebook.com/elisefaberauthor

a amazon.com/author/elisefaber

BB bookbub.com/profile/elise-faber

O instagram.com/elisefaber

g goodreads.com/elisefaber

P pinterest.com/elisefaberwrite

'pod-product-compliance

`3

→ 9 2 0 2 4 *